TEN THICK INCHES

Also by Kenneth Harrison

Bad Behavior

*Daddy's Boys**

*Lies and Deceptions***

*Young, Hung and Ready for Action**

*erotica

** Published by Seventh Window Publications

TEN THICK INCHES

Erotic Short Stories

Seventh Window Publications

Some of these stories first appeared in somewhat different form in: Blueboy, In Touch and Playguy.

First edition: 2002

Published in the United States of America by:
Seventh Window Publications
P.O. BOX 603165
Providence, RI 02906-0165

ISBN: 0-9717089-1-6

CONTENTS

AN ACTOR'S JOURNAL 7
SUCKING HOSE 23
HIS BEST FRIEND'S DAD 37
SCRATCHING THE ITCH 51
TEN THICK INCHES 59
BEAT THE DRUM 81
BODIES IN MOTION 91
UPLOAD 105
HANGING OUT 121
MASETTO 133

AN ACTOR'S JOURNAL

July 17, 2000

I've been jerking off thinking about Anthony Brusco ever since I started this project. Anthony Brusco, the nineteen year old actor who looked no older than sixteen. The same actor it seemed that everyone across America wanted to have lying naked beside them. The exact Anthony Brusco I used to snicker about when guys I knew talked about how hot he was. But that had been before I saw the film that made him, *Midnight Oasis*.

Seeing Anthony Brusco lying on the beach in nothing but a loin cloth, his youthful body free of hair, his deep blue eyes captivating my imagination and driving me wild with lust. In *Midnight Oasis* his blond hair always looked wind swept, his lips were always in a pout, and even when he was fighting off hunger, snakes and natives he appeared helpless. It was a look that captivated the hearts and groins of Americans everywhere, even the most die hard anti-romantic. Yes, even I fell for his charm.

And so now here I am, a man of forty-four, drooling over

him and trying to appear calm and collected every minute. I'm playing his father in this new film about the relationship between a father and his son.

It's getting more and more difficult not to pop a boner on the set when I'm with the kid. I mean, shit, I take one look into his blue eyes, those full lips and soft blond hair and it's over. My cock just responds. I want to slip my thick seven inches of uncut meat between those lips and watch him suck me off. What I wouldn't do to feel his smooth, wet tongue running along the bottom of my shaft and see it slip in and out of his face. Those eyes looking up at me as he greedily slurps up my prick! If only I knew if I had a chance to score the kid.

Anthony's sexual preferences are unknown to everyone, including the director, Steven Trinque. Steven likes younger guys. When I asked him about Anthony he just laughed, then ran his hand through the salt and pepper mop of hair on his head and said he didn't know. Back then I thought my lusting after the boy would pass, but it didn't. It's probably from being stuck in this small New England town that I can't even find on a map.

Why do they always want to shoot these types of family films in locales that nobody has ever heard of. They always seem to want a generic spot, some place that will appeal to the widest range of viewers possible. Someplace that will remind every adult of their childhood. It seems as if everyone in this small town is awed that we're here. We get spotted walking down the street and all eyes are on us, like we don't have a right to privacy. At least in cities people are less obvious about staring. It's not always easy to pretend you don't notice it when people are pointing you out to their friends.

We're filming a beach scene today, I can't imagine how beautiful Anthony must look in a bathing suit. How I'm going to control myself is beyond me.

Same day, 11:38 p.m.

The shoot on the beach was amazing. Wardrobe put Anthony Brusco in a pair of red and blue bathing trunks that made his lean, hairless form appear more youthful than ever. My bathing trunks were an olive drab that Felice in wardrobe said went well with my complexion.

"The cut accents your firm stomach and hairy chest, making you appear fatherly," Felice said as his brown eyes danced over my torso. Tall and slender, Felice wore his clothes tight, to accent every toned feature he had.

"In all my years of acting, I never thought I would have to look fatherly," I said.

"Don't you worry, some people like that look. You never know what you might get," Felice said as he walked around me to make sure he liked exactly how the trunks fit.

I waited for Felice's final approval, then went to start shooting the scene.

During breaks Anthony sat on the beach and pushed his toes into the sand, his hands placed firmly on the ground behind him. He looked up at the clear blue sky. The director and writer were arguing over one of Anthony's lines, which the director thought was too corny. Trying to keep away from Anthony, I stayed in my chair under the tarp used for shade, which made make-up happy since they didn't want anyone getting more tan than they already were. Continuity and all that.

Finally we did the shoot, which meant I had to slowly walk along the beach while the surf swept over our feet. Anthony said his lines, explaining how upset he was to know his mother was in drug rehabilitation, and how he wished I hadn't tried to hide it from him. I put my arm around him, feeling the heat from his body in my grasp and tried to forget about the cameraman in front of us on the dolly. Surf pounded against the shoreline as we walked. Anthony's face was so close to my chest and I felt his hot breath move the hair on my upper pectorals. It was almost disturbing that I was getting excited by Anthony while playing the role of his father. But it's only a role and not real. Not only that, but who wouldn't get aroused having such a handsome young man walking with you on the beach.

We finished the shoot, then I headed back to the trailer to change. Anthony walked up behind me and slapped his hand on my back. "Good scene there, daddy-o!" he said with a playful grin and a wink before running off to his trailer. Anthony rubbed his hand against his bare chest, his eyes sparkling in the light of day.

This is going smoother than I'd expected, I thought, then disappeared inside the trailer for a little time to regain my composure.

Once inside, my dick started to plump up. I still can't believe that young man was making me so horny. I kept telling myself that he was more than half my age, but it wasn't any use. I kept wondering about the smoothness of his skin and how his lips would feel pressed against mine. What would it feel like to hold his naked body against mine? And would he let out a sigh when I touched his hard cock?

I paced the cramped confines of the trailer trying to stop thinking about Anthony, but it was of little use. All I could think about was how he'd called me daddy-o. I closed my eyes and saw his lithe body once more. His smile, his lips, his eyes, his smooth, nubile torso.

Daddy-o, I could almost hear him saying it! Did Anthony know how seductive he'd made it sound?

I dropped onto the sofa, let out a sigh and stretched out my legs. My dick was hard and aching for a little attention, so I reached in and pulled it out. With my eyes closed, I tried to think of something sexual that did not involve Anthony Brusco, but that wasn't going to happen. All I could conjure up was his image, close to me. Anthony's hand on my ass, mine on his.

As everyone knows, Anthony has an amazingly formed ass, perfectly rounded. I imagined how nice it would be to go down on my knees, pull down his shorts and run my tongue along the crack of his ass. I couldn't imagine what his hole would taste like, but wished I could find out. If only I could tickle his tight pucker with the tip of my tongue, getting it wet and ready for my fingers to push their way inside. I couldn't help but think about getting Anthony's fuck hole ready for my cock. How nice it would be to unroll a condom over my dick then slip it up his ass. The thought of Anthony's sphincter gripping my shaft while it pistons in and out of him was just enough to make me blow my load.

I'm getting all excited again as I write this. My hand furtively reaches down between my legs, and I wrap my fingers around my big hairy balls. It feels good when I pull down on them and wish it was Anthony on his knees in front of me, sucking on my nuts. I'll have to spend another night alone, jerking off.

July 18, 2000

Finally, some sexual release! Although it wasn't with Anthony, hopefully it will be enough to keep sexual thoughts of Anthony from my mind. I say that despite the fact that I know it will take much more than one night of libidinous pleasure to do that. I'll tell you all about my hot sex in a minute, but let me explain my day first.

We were shooting yet another outdoor scene, this time in a park. Steven seems to have a thing for the great outdoors. Every chance we get to shoot in the open air, he takes. It's such a beautiful summer that I don't really mind so much. Nothing but clear blue sky and warm sun. Everyone in make-up keeps bitching about it, though. I don't know how they think everyone is going to stay pale when we're outside all the time. I heard one of the make-up men telling Steve that we need more shaded areas for the actors to hang out under while they're waiting for their scenes. Steven said he'd see what he could do, which is as good as saying he thought there was enough shade.

During one of the breaks I stopped for an ice coffee at the catering table. Anthony came up to me and hung around some, taking his time stirring his ice coffee. He'd put in some cream, stir it, then bring the rim of the cup up to his full lips and take a sip. Then he'd put it down, add a little more cream, and do the same thing all over again. He only did it a few times, but it seemed to take him forever to get his ice coffee right. It isn't even good ice coffee, so why he went to all the trouble was beyond me. But I didn't mind watching, especially once he put the cover on the cup and poked a straw through the hole. His lips gripped the straw as he sucked the cold liquid inside the cup.

I turned away from him and drank my coffee as if looking over at the cameramen as they got things ready for us to join them on the next shot.

"Sometimes I really just want to cut out of here and head home," Anthony said.

I turned to look at him, thinking his beauty wouldn't bother me. I was wrong.

"You ever feel that way?" Anthony asked.

"Sure," I said, looking away from his innocent seduction. "It's the monotony of taking a day to repeat the same lines over and over again with a camera constantly in front of you."

Anthony contemplated what I'd told him, then said, "After this I'm taking a break. My manager thinks it's a mistake, but I don't care."

"Everyone needs a break," I said. "Where would you go?"

"I'm thinking of the Caribbean, or some place exotic like that," he said before placing the straw against his lips and taking a sip of coffee while looking at me. He swallowed. "I would like to go someplace where I can just take off all my clothes and run around with my privates flapping free."

Images of Anthony running naked amongst surf and sand shot into my head faster than a speeding locomotive. My cock was quick to respond, so I was forced to push my hands into my pockets. I quickly changed the topic to the shoot schedule, and general Hollywood gossip. As it turned out, Anthony was up on who was doing what.

Steven called Anthony over. Just as he was about to walk off, Anthony turned to me and said that for once he'd like to be able to live and not worry about what might get out. He'd said it so casually, as if it had been an afterthought, that I hadn't given it much weight.

Felice sauntered past me, his eyes festively passing over my crotch, and said hello. Since Felice didn't drop by to chat, I assumed he was heading elsewhere.

By the time the day was done I was horny as hell. I sat on my bed at the far end of the cramped confines of my trailer and kicked off my loafers. As much as I hated jerking off again, I didn't feel like scouting through this small New England town searching for a gay bar. I was tired and horny and just wanted to get off.

There was a knock on the door. I told whoever it was to enter, then the door opened a crack and I saw Felice's grinning face peer into the doorway. He stepped inside, apologizing for intruding on my privacy, then dropped on the hardback chair sitting in front of the desk to my left. "I was wondering if perhaps you know of a bar in the area," Felice said. "A bar that is perhaps my type, you know." He grinned, exposing perfectly white teeth.

I stood, then made my way towards the desk and leaned my ass against it. "Things getting too much for you out in the middle of nowhere?" I asked, knowing that the outline of my shaft was prominent.

Felice turned towards me, eyed my crotch, then looked up. "I see you understand," he said, then reached up and placed the slender fingers of his right hand against my bulging prick.

"You'd be able to see better if you took it out," I said.

Felice feigned surprise, then fell to his knees, opened my fly and lugged out my stiff cock. Felice pulled my hairy nuts out of the fly, then wrapped his fingers around them. He gently tugged on my balls and his lips slid over my ripe cock head. I grabbed the back of his head and slammed my meat down his hungry throat in one fell swoop. Felice didn't even gag as he gulped down every inch of my meat. His brown eyes opened wide as my slick, fleshy tube pistoned in and out of his eager lips. How I wanted to pull my cock out of his mouth and let my load pulse onto his face, covering his face with thick cum. I wanted to watch my spunk shoot onto his nose and drip off his chin, but I held back. I wanted to enjoy this sexual foray. Who knew when there would be another?

I pulled my prick out of his mouth, watching as a thin strand of spit connected the head of my cock with his beautiful mouth. "Come up here," I said, then unbuttoned his thin cotton shirt, exposing his narrow chest. I ran my white hands over his dark Latino flesh, pushing my thumbs against his nickel sized nipples. Felice slipped his shirt off his shoulders and let it flow down his back, then land in a soft pile on the floor. I wanted to see his naked form in front of me, so I undid his pants and let them drop at his feet. Felice kicked off his sandals, then stepped out of his pants. He stood in front of me, his stiff dick rising up long and thin, the hooded cowl covering half his bulbous cock head. His big balls hung low in his sagging sack, and swayed when he shifted from right foot to left.

I took off my clothes, then stepped up to him and ran my hands over his smooth chest, feeling the slender contour of his body. Felice's hands did the same to me, then we kissed long and deep. And as we kissed, my hands roamed Felice's back, gliding over his firm ass, my fingertips dipping into the crack. Felice parted his legs and I rubbed his tight pucker with my middle finger.

"Man, that feels good," Felice whispered as he pressed his stiff dick against my hip and started rubbing.

Slowly, I went down on my knees, slipped the head of his prick into my mouth and sucked. Felice let out a gasp as his knob swelled in my mouth. With one hand, I grabbed the length of his six inch rod and wrapped the fingers of my free hand around his sack. I gently tugged on his nuts. The musty scent of his ass was still on my finger, and I was able to catch traces of it with each inhale. How nice it would be to lick Anthony's hole, I thought as Felice's breathing became more labored.

"You have to stop or I will cum," Felice said.

Felice didn't know it, but that was what I wanted. I wanted him to blow a thick creamy load all over my face, then I wanted to beat off as I rimmed his hole. I pulled his cock head out of my mouth and gave the shaft a few strokes, watching the head play peek-a-boo while the fleshy hood rose and fell over it. A thin line of pre-cum drooled out of the piss slit, then Felice let out a groan. His body jerked, and a thick glob of hot spunk shot out of his piss slit and hit my chin. I lifted my head up to let the thick fuck juice dribble down my neck, then another shot splashed on my left cheek. The next blast hit the bridge of my nose and the final shots dribbled out onto my fingers as they gripped his shaft.

Felice looked down at me, his spunk dripping down my face, and I lay back on the floor. "Sit on my face," I said.

Felice straddled my face so he was facing my cock. I watched his firm dark ass make its descent, and the tight puckered hole wink at me. I grabbed his ass, then rubbed my face in his sweet smelling crack before sticking out my tongue and sliding the flat of it against his hole. And as I ate out Felice's fuck hole, I felt his mouth engulf my shaft once more and start working it up to a frothy load. My tongue tickled his tight, wrinkled asshole as he blew me. Then, as I was about to cum, he gripped my shaft and stroked me off to orgasm.

Spent and happy, Felice said he would drop in on me again some time soon, and I told him to feel free. It wasn't sex with Anthony Brusco, but it was good sex and I hope it was enough to make me less horny when I see Anthony again.

July 19, 2000

Despite having had sex yesterday, I woke up today with a raging hardon and last night's dream fresh in my mind. Although pleasant, the dream was of Anthony walking naked into my bedroom and stroking his big dick. Unable to move, I watched Anthony rubbing his smooth chest, stroking his massive shaft and taunting me.

"I know you want it, daddy-o," he said. "Just take it. Come on, touch it. You would like that, wouldn't you? You'd love to suck my cock, maybe even have me blow a load on your face. I can tell. So come on and get it."

I tried to speak, but no words would form. All I could do was watch as Anthony waved his cock at me and touched himself, grinning, telling me to take it; that I could have it as long as I reached out and went for it.

I woke up with my heart racing and my cock hard as a rock. Closing my eyes, I tried to shake off the memory of the dream, but it refused to go away. Taking hold of my shaft, I began to tell myself that there was no way I could approach Anthony for anything but camaraderie. There couldn't be any way that Anthony could know how seductive he was. Seduction was something that just came naturally to him, which was half the reason for his success. I just had to realize it, make due with my imagination and wait until this film is finished shooting.

Same day, 10:46 p.m.

We're beginning to wrap up the film, and the final shoots seem to be going well. I noticed that Anthony has been looking a little haggard, as if the schedule is beginning to wear on him. We shot a scene in a car today, me in the driver's seat and Anthony in the passenger's. The camera was in front of us, where the windshield should be. Steven was talking to a few of the cameramen, lining up the perfect shot, which left me and Anthony alone in the car.

"I'm sick of being in the middle of nowhere," Anthony said, pouting his lips. "I haven't had any real fun since I got here."

Gripping the steering wheel, I turned towards him and grinned and said, "I know just how you feel."

"At least you can head out to a club or something. That is, if they have any that are fun. Not that I can go, even though I'm nineteen."

"I haven't found any, so you're not missing anything," I said, ruffling up his hair to try and make him smile.

"What do you think I am, your little boy," Anthony said, batting my hand away. He gave me a sideways glance and a dirty grin.

"I don't have a son."

Anthony crossed his arms, then said, "I figured that out."

"A few more days and we're out of here," I said.

Anthony nodded, keeping his arms crossed. "How about dropping by my hotel room tonight to run through some lines?"

"Everyone in their places!" Steven called out before I had a chance to say yes.

The rest of the day went well, and I had expected that Anthony would let his invitation go to the wayside. Thankfully I was wrong. At the end of the day he walked up to me and asked what time I was going to drop in on him.

"Sometime after dinner," I said.

I was eager to be alone with Anthony in his hotel room,

and was afraid it showed more and more as the day went on.

By the time I got back to my hotel room my shaft was rock hard and not about to go down any time soon. I didn't want to be alone with Anthony and start drooling, so I thought it would be best to jerk off before throwing on a pair of shorts, a t-shirt and sandals, then heading out to meet him.

The hotel where Anthony was staying was four blocks away from mine. He had a deluxe suite on the top floor, overlooking the ocean. I went up to the top floor, knocked on the door, them stuffed my hands in my pockets and waited.

Anthony was wet, with a towel wrapped around his waist, as he answered the door to his hotel room. His hair was tossed around as if he'd just rubbed it dry with a towel.

"I'm running late," Anthony said as I stepped inside. The living room was tasteful, with a beige leather sofa and mahogany coffee and end tables. Anthony's pale feet hit the deep pile rug as he searched the room, securely gripping the towel around his waist to keep it from falling. My imagination was running wild, and the excitement of seeing Anthony Brusco wet and half naked was sexy enough to get my prick to respond.

"Would you like anything to drink?" Anthony asked, looking me over. "The room has a mini-bar."

"No, no thank you," I said, knowing that it would not be a good thing to loosen my inhibitions.

Anthony shrugged, then said, "Well, I still need to change. Why don't you take a seat on the sofa."

So I slipped off my sandals, then sat on the sofa. At first I thought everything would work out fine, then Anthony sat down next to me, spread his legs and let the towel fall open. And there it was, rising up a good eight inches between his legs, Anthony Brusco's cock. I tried not to look, but couldn't help taking a gander at his prick.

Anthony reached between his legs and cupped his tight nut sac. "Does it bother you to see your on screen son naked?" he asked.

My cock was getting stiffer by the moment as Anthony sat beside me, waiting for a response. I didn't know what to say, so I sat there like a stupid drone waiting for something to happen.

"Does that mean no?" Anthony asked, giving my thigh a firm pat before leaving his hand on my leg. Anthony's gaze went to my bulging hardon, then he looked up at me again and smiled. Slowly, Anthony's hand slid up my thigh, his fingers dipping inside the leg of my shorts until the tips of his fingers were brushing against the head of my cock.

"I think daddy-o likes it," Anthony said. He looked straight at me and grinned. "Am I being bad?"

I shook my head, then grabbed hold of Anthony's shaft, feeling its girth in my grip. I gave it a few strokes, watching as Anthony's eyes closed from the pleasure of my hand.

Anthony's hands went from my cock to my shirt, pulling it up over my head then tossing it to the floor. He pressed his face into my chest, inhaled, then started licking and biting my left nipple. Then his lips rose up to my neck, where the tip of his tongue roamed up to my ear.

"Why don't you show your boy what pleasure is," he whispered.

Wrapping my arms around his torso, I held him close to me, then whispered, "Show me what pleasure is first."

Anthony's full lips wrapped around the head of my cock. In one gulp he swallowed the length of my shaft and began to suck on it. I held onto his bobbing head as he gripped the base of my cock and sucked long and hard, getting it ready to explode with a wild burst of hot spunk.

Leaning back, I closed my eyes and enjoyed the pleasure of his hot mouth on my meat. He sucked cock like a pro, using just enough suction and keeping his tongue flat against my stiff rod. He worked the head, getting it ripe and ready. And although I had jerked off before heading to Anthony's hotel room, he had me worked up for a second shot of creamy jizz.

Anthony slipped my prick out of his mouth and looked up at me, his lips wet with spit. "I want you to cum for me," he said.

Not yet, I thought, then told him to get on his back. Anthony did as he was told, then I climbed on top of him in a sixty-nine position. As I leaned over him, Anthony sucked my hairy nuts into his mouth. The boy really knew how to please a man, and I was more than ready to give him a little pleasure in return.

Reaching under Anthony, I pushed his ass up and exposed his tight little pucker. I went down and gave it a little kiss, then watched it wink at me. How sweet, I thought before going back down on it and giving it a good lick. Anthony's legs rose higher, as if begging me to lick his asshole. I put the flat of my tongue against his hole and got it wet with spit, then tickled it with the tip of my tongue.

In return, Anthony spit my balls out of his mouth, then began to rim my fuck hole. He moistened my hole then pulled his arms between my legs and began to finger fuck my ass. I moaned as he inserted two and three fingers up my hole, sliding them in and out. He drove me crazy the way he played with my ass as I licked his.

"Come here," Anthony said as he pulled his fingers out of my hole.

I turned to face him, then gave him a gentle kiss. The scent of my ass was fresh on his lips, so I kissed him again to taste it on his tongue. Anthony grabbed my shaft and started giving it long, smooth strokes as we kissed. I closed my eyes and tried to hold back. Spunk was already filling my shaft, getting ready to burst free. But I didn't want to cum yet. I still wanted to enjoy his naked body and feel the pleasure he was giving me.

Our lips parted. Still holding my cock, Anthony said, "I

want you to shoot your load all over me."

My cock twitched in Anthony's grip. Slowly, he slid his hand up and over my swollen knob then back down. Cum collected at the head of my prick, getting ready to burst. I bit my lip, closed my eyes and tried to hold back.

"Come on, daddy-o, shoot it all over me," Anthony said.

My body tightened. No, I thought, not yet. I opened my eyes and looked straight into his. Then I felt the first wave of hot fuck juice spew from my piss slit and slap Anthony's chest. Another wave of cream shot out and splattered on his stomach. The next shot landed on his left pectoral, and the fourth covered his mid section. The final drops spilled out of my piss slit and landed in Anthony's bush of wiry pubic hair.

Anthony's hand moved from my shaft to his own. I kissed him on the lips, then lower. Anthony's chest rose and fell with his breathing as my tongue ran down the center of his pectorals. I licked up tasty cream on his chest and stomach as he continued to stroke his cock. Sticking my tongue in his navel, I lapped up the thick jizz that had collected there. Then I heard Anthony's breathing become heavy and I knew he was close. His legs twitched, then he let out a soft moan. I wanted to feel his juice spray on my face, so continued to lick his stomach.

"Oh fuck," Anthony whispered, then a wet glob of cum slapped against my right cheek. I waited for the next to shoot, which wasn't far behind. Anthony's legs twitched even more as he emptied his nut juice all over my face. A thin river of spunk dribbled off my chin and onto his stomach as I rose and looked at him.

"You look good," Anthony said, then pulled me towards him. We kissed once more, deep and passionate. Our lips parted, then he reached up and smoothed his fingers through the spunk on my face, and down my neck.

"Why don't you come on vacation with me," Anthony said. "You could probably use a rest."

"Is that really what you want?" I asked.

"It's all I've wanted since we met," he said.

Tomorrow we decide on a vacation getaway, then head off together. I still can't believe this is happening to me.

SUCKING HOSE

Ed tried to concentrate on his cards, but every time he looked up all he could see were Dale's full lips. Why the fuck did a boy like Dale get put in this department? Dale couldn't be any older than twenty-two. The kid's eyelashes were longer than any he'd ever seen, and that short dark hair was just long enough for Ed to wrap his thick, rough fingers in to hold the kid's head still while he plowed his mouth good. Ed liked nothing more than feeling his shaft sliding against a tongue as it plunged down some guy's throat. It was even better if the guy whose face he was fucking started to gag. Ed had always said that if you can't swallow his cock you shouldn't try to suck it.

How would Dale do sucking his bone? Ed couldn't help but wonder about it. He could almost see the little pig on his knees sucking cock. Now that would be a pretty picture, he thought. He imagined what Dale would look like with spit dripping off the sides of his mouth while his face was crammed full of stiff meat. Thinking about slipping his prick into Dale's pretty mouth was getting Ed's dick harder by the minute.

He glanced at the scattered dollars and change in the pot, then up at Neil's ugly mug. Neil had the nose of a boxer that had been hit in the face one too many times, and the scar that ran from the right side of his nose to the corner of his mouth made him look even more severe. And if that wasn't enough, Neil's bald head added to the fright factor, making him look creepy enough to scare even Ed if he'd run into the guy in a dark alley.

Jake started drumming his long fingers on the table top, then cleared his throat. "Come on Ed, it's time to shit or get off the pot," Jake said, his voice scratchy as ever. He ran his fingers down the creases on either side of his mouth, then let out a sigh.

Ed had nothing, and, thanks to fucking Dale, he'd taken too long to try to bluff. He threw his cards face down on the table, then leaned back in his chair. "Fuck this shit," he said.

"You having a hard time concentrating?" Jake said, batting his baby blues as he gave Ed a dirty grin. "Seems to me like you've got something on your mind."

Ed chucked Jake the bird, then tilted his chair back. Jake knew what was on Ed's mind. Jake had even told Ed how he'd been wanting to get his cock in Dale's mouth, too. He'd even mentioned that maybe if Dale was into it, the two of them could plow him. Ed hoped he'd get the first shot at stuffing the kid's mouth full of his hefty eight inch beef stick. He wanted to feel his big hairy nut sac smacking against that boy's chin, and his shaft sliding down his warm, moist gullet. Ed rubbed his hands on his jeans, feeling the thick tube of flesh getting harder by the minute.

Neil tossed another bill in the pot, then eyeballed Dale before raising the ante another buck. "Well, son, what are you going to do?" Neil asked.

Dale folded his cards up, then placed the pile face down in

front of himself. Leaning forward, he met Neil's stare. Ed knew there was going to be trouble. Dale was too new to the group to be acting so damn cocky, especially with Neil. And Ed thought Neil had something decent in his hand this time around. If Neil was bluffing he'd have raised the bid up by another fifty cents or so. Dale sat up, then glanced over at Jake before shifting his stare to Ed.

"Don't go looking at me for answers," Ed said. "You want to be a big boy, you play like a big boy."

"And I think it's far time you showed us something, 'cause I'm damn sick of looking at that pretty face of yours," Jake said, the right corner of his mouth curled in a smirk.

Looking at his cards, Dale bit his bottom lip, then slid down in his chair. All eyes were on him and he knew it. Holding his cards in his left hand, he reached his right hand out and pushed two dollars into the pot. He looked up, then tossed in another dollar. He folded his cards, put them face down on the table, sat up straight and leered at both Neil and Jake.

Ed looked at Dale, so cocky in his innocence. He hoped the littler fucker knew what he was doing. Neil's eyes bugged out while Jake looked down at the pot then back up at Dale. He shook his head.

"You can take that back, since you don't know what you're doing," Jake said.

Dale blew Jake a kiss, then said, "I'm not taking anything back."

"You fucking cock sucker," Jake said as he looked down at his cards and contemplated his next move. He glanced up at Neil, then down at his cards.

"Afraid the pretty boy might have something, Jake?" Neil asked.

"Fuck you," Jake said as he threw his cards face down the table. "I fold."

Neil threw another dollar into the pot, then glared at Dale

and said, “It’s time.”

“Show me,” Dale said as he slowly laid out his hand, a royal flush.

“You fucking shit!” Neil called out as he threw his cards across the table.

Dale let out a laugh as he scooped the pot towards him.

The fire alarm went off. Ed ran across the room, jumped onto the metal pole with his legs dangling. He quickly slid down the hole to the first floor. He grabbed his heavy fire jacket, then pushed his feet into the rubber boots, gripping the red rubber handles on top of each boot to get his feet comfortable. He ran to where engine #9 waited. Jake, Dale and Neil weren’t far behind, followed closely by Jack and Tim, who had been relaxing in the common bedroom.

By the time Ed had the driver’s side door of the fire engine open and one foot on the step, the other men were getting themselves into position on the truck. Ed sprang inside, checked out his rear view mirror to see Dale waving and grinning to go. The garage door was open. Ed turned the key in the ignition, ran the sirens, then pulled out onto Brook Street.

A single family house on Maple Drive had flames pouring out the second floor windows and licking the light blue siding. People conjugated on the sidewalk, looking up at the burning house as if astonished. A woman in slippers and a housecoat was huddled in an unshaven man’s arms, her face pushed against the thin white t-shirt that hung off his slender frame. The man looked up at the house as if unable to believe his eyes, and Ed knew that it was their house that was burning.

Already Neil and Dale were pulling out the fire hose as Tim opened the fire hydrant at the end of the block, then attached the hose to it. In the second floor window a small black and white long hair cat let out a panicked cry.

The woman pulled herself away from the man she'd been clutching and ran towards the house with her arms outstretched in the air. "Muffin!" she called.

Ed ran up to the woman and took hold of her before she could run frantically into the house. Her arms flailed as she fought him, but he was able to hold her back. The last thing they needed was to have to rescue someone who'd already fled the premises.

"Is this your house, ma'am?" Ed asked.

"Muffin! You have to save him," the woman called out.

The unshaven man who had been with her earlier walked up to them and said, "It's only the cat. The house is empty."

"Save my muffin," the woman screamed as she clutched Ed's arm.

Ed glanced at the front door, which was open. Suited up, Jake walked out the front door and gave the okay. The house was clear and everything was running as it should. Neil wielded the nozzle of the fire hose at the house, spraying it while Tim steadied the hose behind him.

"Muffin," the frantic woman screamed as she pointed up to a second floor window.

Then Ed saw Dale running into the house, axe in hand. What the fuck was that little shit doing? Ed thought, then ran into the house after Dale.

Down the hall, flames leapt up from the floor in what seemed to be the kitchen. To his right, the end of the sofa flickered with red and yellow as the fire rose up the side and extended upwards, towards the wall. There were footsteps above him. The stairs were to his left. Cautiously, he made his way up the steps as the heat of the interior of the house surrounded him. The fire had begun to take over the second story, rising up through the bathroom floor and melting the vinyl shower curtain. Across from him, flames shot through the floor of the bedroom in the rear of the house. Dale appeared in the door to the right, clutching the cat close to his chest.

"We got to get out of here," Dale called out over the crackling flames.

Ed stood back to let Dale pass, then followed him down. He looked back to see the fire reaching up towards the ceiling, then continued down the stairs.

Walking out of the house, he saw Dale's back and heard the woman crying. "Oh thank you!"

Ed walked up to the fire engine and started pulling out a second hose. On the front lawn, the frantic woman clutched the long hair cat close to her face and rocked it back and forth. "Dale, get over here and help me with the hose!" Ed called out.

"Sure thing!" Dale said, then ran up to him.

Rookies were always doing stupid things, Ed thought as he attached the hose to the fire hydrant. Running into a burning building without backup or orders. Sometimes they learned the hard way, sometimes they got off easy; other times they didn't get off at all.

Ed watched Dale run off with the end of the hose. They didn't need another hose, but he wanted to keep Dale busy, which was probably the only way to keep the kid out of trouble. Dale was a real cute fucker, Ed didn't want to see any harm come to him.

Ed and the boys were back at the firehouse. Dale hung up his coat, then pulled off his boots as Neil eyed the table, glancing at their cards. Dale's pretty face was covered with black soot, as was Ed's. Neil stood with his hands on the chair in front of his cards, then turned towards Dale. "Well, you up for another game?"

Dale winked at Ed, then moseyed over towards the table. He resumed gathering his winnings and said, "Are you in a hurry to lose again?"

"Beginner's luck," Neil said as he began collecting the cards. He looked hungrily at Dale, as if he wanted something more than another chance to win his money back.

"What's that look for?" Dale asked. "You in a hurry to get back what was once yours?"

"Maybe," Neil said. "Then again, maybe there's more to it than that."

"Whatever it is, maybe you should calm it down," Dale said. "I need to shower and get some sleep."

Neil turned towards Ed. "Isn't he a cocky little fucker?"

Ed laughed, then walked out of the room. That was the truth, Dale was a cocky little shit. Shaking his head, Ed wondered if Dale knew exactly what he was getting himself into. It seemed the kid just couldn't take himself away from trouble. Sooner or later it was going to catch up to him.

Oh well, he thought, what he needed was a shower. Ed walked past the bedroom, then into the bathroom. He couldn't stop thinking about Dale and how things might catch up to him. If it was sexual, he hoped he would be around when it did happen. The thought put a smile on his face and a stiffness between his legs.

The clean white tiled bathroom always had that slight scent of bleach that drove Ed mad. Sure, he was glad they kept the room spotless, but Neil had to lay off on the disinfectant. He looked at the drain in middle of the bathroom floor, which was spotless, then at the four shower nozzles against the wall. Who would think a house full of guys would have one of the cleanest bathrooms in the country, he thought.

Without closing the bathroom door, Ed started to undress. He peeled off his navy blue firefighter t-shirt, then unbuttoned his jeans and let them fall to the floor. The dark, thick patch of hair on his well developed pecs was damp with sweat, and his big balls were hanging real low from the heat, too. His thick shaft dangled seven inches between his legs. He gave his cock a playful bat with his hand and watched it sway back and forth. He thought about Neil and how Dale had pissed him off by beating the shit out of him at cards. Neil was going to try real hard to figure Dale's game out the next time they all sat down for a game of poker.

He'd forgotten to grab a fresh towel from the closet in the hall, so he stepped out of the bathroom, then opened the narrow closet door to the left of the bathroom door. The top shelf held stacks of clean white towels. He grabbed one, then headed back into the bathroom and got the shower running.

Ed stepped up to the wall with four shower heads lined up, then turned on the water and placed his head under the hot spray. Water seeped into his hair, then ran down his back and over his chest. He grabbed hold of the soap, then started lathering his nuts, rolling the soapy globes between his fingers and tugging down on the sac. His prick stiffened to nine inches, rising hard against his stomach.

He wondered how long it would take before one of the guys came onto Dale. Not only that, but what would happen? Was Dale the kind of guy who liked to suck dick? If not, he would have to make it clear. But Ed thought Dale would get down on his knees if asked. There was just something about the kid, something beyond his arrogance. Dale just seemed too comfortable around a bunch of guys who looked at him with lust in their eyes. If he was right and Dale liked to get it on with men, he hoped he'd get a chance to slip his meat between that boy's lips. What he wouldn't give to watch Dale choke on his fucking beef stick.

"Hey there," Dale said as he walked into the bathroom with a green towel wrapped around his waist, his bare feet slapping against the tiled floor. Dale's smooth, lean body was damp with sweat and dark patches of soot were still on his face. He took off his towel and threw it on one of the sinks. Dale's uncut cock stuck out between his legs, bobbing and swaying as he stepped up to the shower head to the right of

Ed. Before turning on the shower, he looked down at Ed's boner and smirked.

"What, you never seen a hardon?" Ed said.

"Maybe you should have taken care of things before your shower. You don't want anyone to get the wrong impression," Dale said.

"At least I don't give the impression of being a fool."

Dale ignored Ed's comment.

"You could have been killed today, you know," Ed said.

"I have a thing for animals," Dale said. "They are living things, you know."

Ed rolled his eyes. He didn't need to hear this from a rookie. "But you went in alone, and without telling anyone. You don't do that."

Dale turned and let the water cascade off his smooth back and firm ass. Ed was going nuts. He wanted to go down and bite that boy's butt in the worst way. Instead he gave it a slap.

"Hey!" Dale said, his voice reverberating off the tile. "What the fuck did you go and do that for?" He turned around, his boner rising up high and mighty.

"Looks like you enjoyed it," Jake said, leaning in the doorway to the bathroom with his arms folded, a towel tossed over his left shoulder. His firm chest had a sprinkling of hair, and his cock and balls dangled soft and low between his legs.

"Fuck you, Jake," Dale said, then turned away from the two men and started soaping his arm pits. "It happens, is all."

"Don't I know that," Ed said, trying hard not to laugh.

Jake threw his towel on the row of sinks, then stepped up to Ed and placed his hand against his hairy ass. "I didn't say it was anything to be embarrassed about," he said. "Shit, I've seen good old Ed's chubby a few times up close."

Ed turned to face Jake and grabbed Jake's thick tube steak, feeling it stiffen to ten inches in his grip. "Sometimes a guy just needs a little help with his hose."

"Isn't that the truth," Jake said, then slapped Dale's ass.

Dale turned, looking shocked as hell to see Ed stroking Jake's meat. He glanced at the open door, then at Ed, then Ed's fist pumping away at Jake's cock. His eyes widened, and he hungrily licked his full lips.

"We're not doing anything anyone else here hasn't done, so don't go looking so surprised," Ed said. He reached out and rubbed the back of his hand against Dale's firm dick.

Dale didn't move. He didn't even flinch. Instead his face turned slightly red and he closed his eyes.

"That feels nice," Dale said. "It's been a while since I've done anything like this." He stepped forward and slipped his arm around Ed's waist, then leaned in and gave him a sweet kiss on the lips. No tongues, just lip against lip.

"So, you like it when a guy touches your dick," Ed said softly.

"I don't mind it," Dale said.

"How do you feel about pleasuring another guy?" Ed asked.

Dale was silent as he looked at Ed.

Jake walked up behind Dale and said, "Taking his fat cock in your mouth and sucking away on it, would you like that?"

Ed stared at Dale, pleased to see the cocky little fuck squirm a little. He looked down and saw Dale's hard shaft twitch. "I bet you would like that," he said. "I can see you sucking my cock."

Dale looked down at Ed's prick, then went down on his knees. Jake walked up beside him and watched as Dale wrapped his lips around the crown of Ed's cock head. Reaching out, Ed took hold of Jake's shaft and gave it a squeeze as he felt his shaft ease down Dale's warm, moist gullet. He couldn't believe what an expert cock sucker Dale was.

"That's fucking beautiful," Jake said, watching as Dale's head bobbed up and down on Ed's prick.

With his eyes closed, Ed felt Dale grab hold of the base of

his shaft and work the head over, sucking long and hard on it. Dale's lips rubbed ever so gently along the swollen knob before gliding back down on the shaft once more. Dale's tongue slid over the bottom of Ed's prick as he eased his mouth up his mighty beef stick. Again Dale worked the head, making it swell and beg for Ed to let loose with a load of hot spunk.

"Oh fuck, not yet," Ed hissed, then let go of Jake's meat. He opened his eyes and watched as Dale pulled his mouth off his cock and started swallowing Jake's pud.

Jake let out a moan as Dale swallowed his meat in one smooth gulp. Dale was a fucking pro at sucking cock, Ed thought as he slipped his fingers through Dale's wet hair, guiding his bobbing head on Jake's cock. Dale's nose went straight to Jake's pubic hair, paused, then slid back up Jake's love muscle again.

Jake slapped Ed's ass, then let his hand stay on his hairy butt cheeks. He leaned in and licked Ed's lips. But Ed didn't let Jake go so fast. He wrapped his free hand around Jake's waist, pulled him in close and gave him an open mouth kiss. Their tongues slid over one another, then he felt Dale start going at his prick again. The boy didn't lay up, not for a minute. Ed stepped back, then pulled Dale's face off his prick.

"Man, you keep working it like that and I'll start spurting my load all over you," Ed said.

"That's fine with me," Dale said with a dirty grin, then slipped Ed's right nut into his mouth and started sucking on it.

Ed closed his eyes and concentrated on Dale. When he opened his eyes, he saw Neil standing in the doorway.

"That's one fucking horny bastard," Neil said, standing in the doorway with his thin, semi hard shaft in his fist. A bead of pre-cum glistened on the tip of the purple knob, then dripped onto the floor. Neil slid his hand over his smooth, narrow chest, then padded into the bathroom and stood in front of Dale.

Ed let out a grunt as Dale sucked his left ball into his mouth along with the right and closed his lips around them. All Dale had to do to make him blow his load was touch his cock, Ed was that excited.

Dale reached out and grabbed Neil's prick with his left hand and Jake's with his right. Ed looked down and met Dale's gaze. He wanted to blow his load on Dale's beautiful face so damn bad, but still wanted to enjoy the boy while he could. Reaching down, he pressed his shaft against the side of Dale's nose, then rubbed it over the bridge. It felt so good that he almost lost his load right then and there.

"Oh fuck," Jake called out through clenched teeth.

Ed slapped his meat against Dale's face as he watched Jake's knees buckle. Jake let out another groan as Dale's fist continued to stroke his prick.

"Oh yes," Jake said, "I'm so fucking close."

Dale let go of Neil's dick, then spit Ed's nuts out of his mouth as a thin line of drool spilled out over his lower lip. Positioning his face closer to Jake's swollen knob, Dale continued to stroke. Jake let out a grunt, and the first glob of hot spunk shot out of his piss slit and splattered against Dale's smooth cheek. The second shot rang out and fell close to the first. Dale turned his face and let the other side get covered with Jake's creamy spunk.

Ed couldn't take his eyes off Dale's cum drenched face. How fucking pretty, he thought as he wrapped his fingers around his stiff cock. Knowing it wouldn't take more than a stroke or two before he shot, he kept his hand still. There would be plenty of time to shoot his load.

Turning towards Neil, cum dripping off his chin, Dale reached out and grabbed Neil's stiff dick. Slowly, he slid it into his mouth and started sucking it like a cock hungry pig.

"Oh man," Neil said, "this one's a keeper."

Ed watched Dale slide Neil's shaft in and out of his mouth. Then he felt Dale's hand reach out, so he let go of his meat and let Dale have at it. Dale gave it one downward stroke, then slid his hand up over the head, then back down as he continued to suck Neil's dick. Ed's knees buckled as his body tightened. He closed his eyes, then felt the pressure building up in his cock head. It was going to be soon and he knew it. Looking down, he saw Dale's head still bobbing on Neil's shaft. Dale's hand slid up and over the head of his cock once more, then a hot blast of cream spurted out of Ed's piss slit and slapped against the side of Dale's lovely face. Ed let out a grunt, and another shot spurted out of his pulsing cock head and landed on Dale's neck. The next hit his shoulder.

"Oh man, I'm going to fucking loose it," Neil said.

Dale grabbed hold of Neil's shaft, then slid the pole out of his mouth and started stroking it. Neil's purple knob oozed thick, clear pre-cum with each stroke before it spewed its load on Dale's forehead and nose, dripping off the tip and landing on his chin.

When Neil's cock had finished spitting out the final drops of spunk, Dale rubbed the thick fuck juice into his face and neck, then lay down on the tiled floor. All three men stood around the boy as he used the cream as lube to stroke his prick. Dale pulled on his nuts with his right hand, keeping his legs spread as he stroked his shaft. After four strokes Dale's breathing became heavy, reverberating off the tiled walls and floor of the bathroom. But it wasn't until Dale's knees rose up, and his toes curled that it seemed he would shoot. Ed looked at Dale's full lips, which were parted ever so slightly, then Dale's head pushed back, his eyes rolled upwards, and a thick burst of jizz spurt out of his piss slit and hit his stomach.

"Oh fuck," Jake whispered.

Another shot sprang out of Dale's cock and landed with a splat between his pecs. Dale let out a groan, then his body twitched, and shot a second load onto his stomach. The remainder of his spunk spewed from his piss slit, covering his stomach and filling his navel.

"Oh man, that was great," Jake said when Dale had finished shooting his load.

Ed reached out for Dale to take his hand, then pulled him to his feet. "Guess you're going to make it," he said.

"I never had a doubt about that," Dale said.

HIS BEST FRIEND'S DAD

It was the last summer Danny and Tim would spend together. They'd spent their high school years as best friends, now they were eighteen and getting ready to head off to colleges on opposite ends of the country. They'd decided to make the most of their final summer together. Because of that, everything they did seem tinged with importance. From tennis, to swimming, to a simple game of catch, everything they did felt as if it might just be the last time they did it. But for Danny, what he would miss most was going out for bike rides with Tim Valenski and his father.

Mr. Valenski was tall, with dark curly hair that sometimes dropped down to just above his eyebrows, a downward sloped nose and strong chin that made him look like a boxer. His well defined chest was covered with a thick patch of hair that tapered down to a thin line that separated the two halves of his tight stomach and disappeared beneath the waistband of his pants. And between his legs, no matter what he wore, there was the prominent bulge that could only mean he had a hefty package.

The first time Danny had seen Tim with his dad he hadn't thought they were father and son. Except for his nose, there was nothing about Tim that would make anyone think they were related. Tim's fair skin and strawberry blond hair came from his mother's side of the family, which bothered Tim since his mother had run out on Tim and his father when Tim was nine years old. Danny had met Tim when they were in their freshman year of high school and had only seen pictures of Tim's mom, but never mentioned the resemblance. It had always been too obvious how Tim felt about the way he looked.

Casually peddling along the blacktop of the bike path with Tim to Danny's right and Mr. Valenski ahead of them allowed time for Danny to contemplate the time he'd spent with Tim and his father. Mr. Valenski rode ahead of them with his shirt off and his muscular legs pumping the peddles of his bike as the three of them rode past assorted trees and bushes. Danny couldn't help but watch Mr. Valenski's beautiful ass rising up from the seat every time he tried to gain speed.

The bike path wove around a group of thick bushes, then went uphill. The chain on Tim's bike clicked as he downshifted. Danny only went down to fifth gear so he could keep up with Mr. Valenski, whose firm ass was riding high above the seat of his bike. The path curved to the right at the top, then straightened out and went downhill. At the bottom there was a sharp left turn. Reaching the top of the hill, Danny kept his fingertips poised and ready to use the breaks if he needed to lose speed on his way down. Coasting downhill, Mr. Valenski turned to look back, his dark brown curls dancing in the breeze as he winked at Danny. Danny felt his dick stir as both he and Mr. Valenksi made a wide left turn at the bottom of the hill.

"Come on, I'll race you!" Tim called out as he sped up on Danny, then passed him.

"No way!" Danny yelled and shifted into eighth gear. The chain switched tracks with a metal clicking and Danny pushed down hard on the peddles to gain enough speed to catch up to Tim. Mr. Valenski was neck and neck with him now. The front tire of Tim's bike was only inches ahead of him. Danny leaned in and peddled harder. Mr. Valenski matched his speed.

Concentrate, Danny thought as he kept his eyes set on the three foot tall stone wall that surrounded the park. He was almost there.

As much as he wanted to, he knew looking to the side could ruin his chances of winning. Tim's bike was just ahead of him, on his right. Danny pumped harder. The entrance was only about eight or so feet away.

Don't look back, Danny thought. He had to concentrate on passing Tim, not on where Mr. Valenski was. Then he heard Tim's squeal of delight as he crossed the line into the park. Danny looked up to see Tim coast into the park, then turn the wheel sharp and skid to a stop.

Danny stopped peddling as he went through the entrance with Mr. Valenski to his left, then stopped his bike and jumped off. Danny's t-shirt was soaked with sweat, so he peeled it off then tucked it into his back pocket the way Mr. Valenski had done before they'd begun riding.

Mr. Valenski patted Danny's back with his big, firm hand. "Good ride, Danny," he said before congratulating Tim with a handshake. "Why don't we take a rest here before heading back."

Mr. Valenski took a seat on the grass and sat with his legs spread and his knees slightly bent. Between his legs, Danny saw the bulge of his meat pushing out against the inside of his shorts. After letting out a sigh, Danny dropped back on the grass, feeling his head against the warm earth. Looking up at clouds set against blue sky he imagined how wonderful it must be to lick Mr. Valenski's sweaty balls, and suck his cock.

A hand slapped Danny's chest, then he heard Mr. Valenski say, "Hey there, tiger, don't get too comfortable."

Danny rolled onto his stomach to hide his stiffening prick. "Don't worry, Mr. Valenski," he said. "I just want to relax for a bit."

Danny's parents were out when he'd arrived home from his bike trip with Tim and his father. He went upstairs to his room and peeled off his shirt, then kicked off his sneakers and tossed them against the wall to the right of the bureau. In the mirror above the bureau he caught his reflection. His body wasn't bad, although it was nothing like Mr. Valenski's. Danny's chest was smooth, his pectorals just barely defined. He hoped that some day he might sprout some chest hair, but didn't think it was all that possible. If he hadn't grown any chest hair by the age of eighteen, he wasn't about to start doing so any time soon.

If only he could be strong and virile like Mr. Valenski. Gliding his fingers through his wiry bush of pubic hair, Danny wondered what Mr. Valenski's pubes were like. Were they thick and coarse like his? And what about his cock? Danny's prick was long and thick, with a tight foreskin that hugged his swollen cock head and only allowed the piss slit to show at the tip when fully erect.

Moving his hand lower, Danny took hold of his hairy nutsac and gave it a tug. He'd seen Tim naked just this past month, when they'd quickly changed into their bathing suits in the men's room at the beach. Tim had big balls that were held close to his body in a tight sack. Tim's cock was long, thin and cut. It dangled just past his nuts. Could Mr. Valenski's cock and balls be similar? Being that Tim looked nothing like his father, Danny didn't think so. After all, would Mr. Valenski's bulge be so prominent if he didn't have a lot of meat in his pants? Mr. Valenski's basket was always ample, the bulge giving the promise of something hefty hidden inside. Plus Danny had seen Mr. Valenski's shaft outlined in his shorts before and it didn't look at all thin.

Moving his hand back to his dick, Danny watched in the mirror as he gripped the thick fleshy tube close to the head, then eased his hand back. The foreskin pulled back, exposing his swollen knob. A pearl of pre-cum formed at the tip, lingered there for a second, then slowly dripped off the tip of his prick and landed on the dresser. He slid his hand back over the shaft and watched as the head was hidden once more in the safe confines of his foreskin.

How good it would be to have Mr. Valenski grabbing his shaft this way, Danny thought as he closed his eyes and recalled their bike ride. In his fantasy things were different. He was alone with Mr. Valenski, the both of them racing to the finish with Danny winning. Then the two of them put their bikes down and relaxed on the grass, a soft breeze drifting over Danny's upper torso as he turned towards Mr. Valenski. Then the feeling of Mr. Valenski's hand on his chest, moving down towards the waistband of his shorts. Danny imagined the feeling of Mr. Valenski's thick fingers holding his cock, grabbing it tight as he slowly moved his fist up and down the length of his rod.

"I want to see you cum," Mr. Valenski whispered, his voice low and masculine.

Yes, Danny thought, feeling the tight grip on his prick. How good it would feel to have Mr. Valenski next to him.

I want to see you cum.

Danny's body tightened, the head of his prick pulsed, then a thick glob of white spunk shot out of his cock and hit the mirror. Another creamy load spewed from his piss slit and hit the top of the bureau. Danny let out a soft moan and spilled the rest of his spunk on top of the bureau.

—

It was Friday night when Danny sat at the kitchen table at the Valenski house playing a game of Gin Rummy with Tim. Tim's father was out with some friends playing pool and doing whatever it was Mr. Valenski did when he went out. Not only did Tim's father rarely discuss what he did on the few nights he went out with his friends, but Tim always made it a point not to ask.

"You don't know where he is?" Danny asked as he looked at his cards and tried to decide what to discard. He chose the four of diamonds.

"He plays pool," Tim said. "There's no big mystery."

Danny nodded as he watched Tim pick up a card from the deck, place it in his hand then study his cards. Already Danny's dick was becoming stiff from the image of Mr. Valenski leaning over a pool table to line up his next shot. Danny had been over before on the nights Mr. Valenski left the house wearing a pair of jeans and a tight t-shirt. He'd always looked so damn hot that Danny wanted to grab his crotch and tell him how bad he wanted to suck his cock.

"Gin!" Tim called out as he placed his point cards on the table.

Danny folded up his hand then threw the cards down. "I can't concentrate."

"That's because you're too curious about things," Tim said. "How about playing some video games, or going for a swim?"

"It's too late," Danny said as he stood and hoped his boner wasn't too noticeable. "I'm not in the mood to swim."

"How about sleeping over? It'll be the last time we'll be able to do it before we head off to college."

"Sure," Danny said, feeling a sad pang at the thought of not being able to spend time with Tim once the two of them went away to school. He called his parents and told them he was spending the night with Tim. After hanging up the telephone, he realized that he might also be able to get a peek at Mr. Valenski with a towel wrapped around his waist in the morning. The thought made his cock tingle.

Danny and Tim went into the living room to play a few video games. After losing two games of Space Infantry to Tim, they went to bed.

Tim was already beneath the soft blue top sheet as Danny stepped out of his shorts and boxers, then pulled off his t-shirt. The room was dark, but his eyes had adjusted, so he was able to see what he was doing as he climbed into bed beside Tim. Tim was silent, his soft breathing wisping through the room.

Danny went onto his back, slid his hands behind his head and closed his eyes. Then he felt the warm touch of a hand on his upper thigh. Was Tim making a move on him? Danny's cock stiffened, then he moved his leg closer to Tim to see what would happen next. Tim's hand slid onto Danny's crotch then began to rub his stiff prick.

Danny slid his hand towards Tim. Tim rolled onto his back, then turned towards Danny and smiled. Danny gripped Tim's thin dick and started slowly stroking it as Tim did the same to him. Closing his eyes, Danny imagined that it was Mr. Valenski next to him, jerking him off. With that in mind, it didn't take long before his body contracted and he blew his load. Tim wasn't far behind.

After the two boys cleaned up with a towel that had been beside the bed, Tim looked over at Danny and smiled. They didn't say anything to each other, not that Danny knew what to say. They'd just jerked each other off and he didn't know exactly what that meant. He hoped Tim wouldn't expect anything more from him, which would make their final days awkward. He didn't want to be anything more than friends with Tim.

Tim rolled over and quickly fell asleep. Danny looked up at the ceiling and tried to sleep. Next to him, Tim began to snore, which was yet another distraction keeping him awake.

Climbing out of bed, Danny slipped into his boxer shorts and made his way downstairs. Luckily he'd been to the Valenski house enough times to be able to make his way downstairs without having to turn on any lights. He went into the dining room, around the large oak table and chairs, then into the kitchen. He hoped they had some milk in the refrigerator.

There was a splash outside. Placing his hands flat against the cool, black marble counter top, he went on tip toes and looked out the small window above the sink. The outline of the pool was in shadow, the rippling surface aglow in moonlight. Then something broke the surface. Someone was swimming in the pool. Whoever it was was doing laps. At the foot of the pool was a pile of something that looked like clothes. Could it be Mr. Valenski? Danny had to find out. Danny walked back into the dining room, then out the sliding glass doors that led to the fenced in backyard. The cement was cool against the bottom of his feet as he walked up to the pool and looked down, watching the figure swim towards him then stop.

"Hey there, Danny," Mr. Valenski said, his arms outstretched to keep himself afloat. "I thought that was your car out front when I got home."

"It got late, so we figured I should just stay the night," Danny said. "Shouldn't you have the pool light on?"

"I don't want to attract attention," Mr. Valenski said as he swam over to the ladder.

Danny slowly nodded.

"Can't sleep?" Mr. Valenski asked.

"Not really. I might just hang out here for a bit if you don't mind."

"Not at all. I was getting out anyhow," Mr. Valenski said as he gripped the metal railing and took a step onto the ladder. Slowly his chest emerged, then his firm stomach and last his long, thick cut cock and big hairy nuts.

Danny took a step back as he watched Mr. Valenski come

out of the pool, then glanced over at the table set off to the side of the house. There were two plastic lawn chairs near the table, one with a towel draped over it. He went over and took a seat on the chair without the towel. Although Danny knew he had to act casual, he wasn't sure he could. The man he'd been lusting over for years was standing around in the buff.

Mr. Valenski was coming closer to him, his pendulous cock dangling between his legs. Danny told himself not to look, but he couldn't help himself. He had to look at it. Water dripped down Mr. Valenski's body and Danny wished he could go down on his knees and lick that water off every inch of him.

Mr. Valenski grabbed the towel off the empty chair next to Danny and began to dry his hair. It was then that Danny knew his boner wasn't about to go down. As the towel shook, so did Mr. Valenski's balls and shaft. Danny couldn't keep his eyes away from Mr. Valenski as he ran the towel under his arms, then dried off his back. He was inches away from Danny, his meat practically in his face. If Danny wanted to touch it all he had to do was reach out.

"Almost ready to go away to college?" Mr. Valenski asked as he ran the towel between his legs, forcing his balls and meat up and over the towel.

"Sure am," Danny said as he looked up at Tim's father. He hoped talking would help his cock go soft. "Tim said you play pool."

The corners of Mr. Valenski's mouth lifted just enough to be called a grin. "Do you play?"

Danny licked his lips, then said, "A little." He glancing in front of him to see that Mr. Valenski's shaft was beginning to stiffen. He looked up. "I haven't had much practice, though."

"Oh, and who do you play with?"

"No one in particular," Danny said. "But I can play."

"Show me," Mr. Valenski said, then looked down at his stiffening prick.

Danny looked briefly at Mr. Valenski's cock, then met his gaze. His face reddened as he swallowed. He couldn't believe his fantasy was about to come true. Danny reached out and grabbed hold of Mr. Valenski's thick, fleshy tube. Leaning forward, he opened his mouth and wrapped his lips around the bulbous head and began to suck on it.

Mr. Valenski softly moaned as he ran his fingers through Danny's hair. Hungrily, Danny began to ease the shaft into his mouth and down his throat. He swallowed, feeling the shaft grow in length as it plumped up, filling his gullet.

"That feels real good," Mr. Valenski said as he slowly moved his hips in a slow fuck. The head of his cock swelled with hot fuck juice as Danny reached between his legs and played with his big hairy balls.

This was what Danny had always wanted, and now it was happening. He had his best friend's father's cock in his mouth. He was sucking Mr. Valenski's massive meat, feeling it fill his throat and stretch his jaw. He had the man's balls in his hands, gently tugging on them. He wished it would never end.

Mr. Valenski stopped fucking Danny's face and pulled out. A thread of spit connected Danny's bottom lip with Mr. Valenski's prick, then broke when Danny went down on his knees and started licking Mr. Valenski's hairy balls. He sucked the right nut into his mouth, then the left and closed his lips around them. Mr. Valenski softly moaned as Danny let both hairy globes pop out from between his lips.

Danny stood and faced him. Mr. Valenski brought his face close to Danny's and gently brushed his lips against Danny's lips. Then Danny felt Mr. Valnski's arms around his waist, rubbing his back, then Mr. Valenski's fingers dipping inside the waist band of his boxer shorts. This was it, this was what Danny had imagined happening to him so many times. He had to keep reminding himself that it wasn't a dream, that it was really happening. Mr. Valenski was holding him, touching him, dipping his fingers in the crack of his ass. Danny parted his legs and felt the tip of Mr. Valenski's thick finger penetrate his hot hole. This was real, Danny thought.

"Why don't you get out of those boxer shorts," Mr. Valenski said, his hot breath brushing against Danny's neck.

Danny slipped his boxers off, then felt Mr. Valenski's hand on his meat, gripping and stroking his shaft. Then Mr. Valenski went down on his knees and turned Danny around so his back was to him. Danny felt Mr. Valenski's fingers part his ass cheeks, exposing his tight pucker. Hot breath rushed over Danny's tight little fuck hole, then the tip of Mr Valenski's tongue tickled his asshole. Danny let out a sigh as Mr. Valenski lapped at his ass with the flat of his tongue, getting it moist with spit.

Mr. Valenski poked his middle finger all the way up Danny's fuck hole, then stood and wrapped his right arm around Danny's chest and pulled him in close. The hair on Mr. Valenski's chest was against Danny's back as he moved his finger in and out of Danny's fuck hole, then pulled it out. Wrapping both arms around Danny, Mr. Valenski slid his shaft up and down the crack of his ass. Closing his eyes, Danny lost himself in the feeling of Mr. Valenski's body pressed against his.

"I've been wanting to feel you naked for so long," Mr. Valenski whispered. "Have you in my arms like this, then spray your chest with my cum."

Danny leaned his head back on Mr. Valenski's shoulder, feeling the man's comforting arm around his upper torso and his meat on his ass crack. The urge to shoot his load made Danny's shaft twitch and his cock head swell.

"I want to see you jerk off," Mr. Vaneski said as he took his left hand and pressed two fingers against Danny's pucker. "I want to feel your asshole contract around my finger as you shoot your load."

Mr. Valenski pulled his fingers out of Danny's hole then

slid it under the his nose. The heady scent of his own ass filled Danny's nostrils.

"Get them wet so I can stick them up your hole," Mr. Valenski said as he poked the same fingers into Danny's mouth.

Danny sucked Mr. Valenski's fingers, tasting his ass as they slid over his tongue and poked down his throat. Both fingers were slippery with spit when they came out of his mouth. Mr. Valenski slid them back up Danny's hole. Danny let out a gasp as they passed his tight ass ring and delved into his bowels.

"Play with yourself," Mr. Valenski said. "I want to see you shoot."

Danny grabbed hold of his prick knowing that it would only take a couple of strokes before he shot. He pushed his ass back, feeling Mr. Valenski's fingers fuck him, then grabbed his rod and began to stroke.

"I can feel your hole get tight," Mr. Valenski whispered as cum built up at the tip of Danny's ripe cock head. "Shoot it."

Danny let out a grunt then felt his legs tighten. He bit his lower lip then let the first blast of hot spooge shoot onto the lawn chair. Mr. Valenki's hold on him got tighter as the second load of jizz shot, then the third. His body jerked and he shot the last of his spunk on the ground at his feet. Danny was still breathing hard when Mr. Valenski pulled his fingers out of his ass. Danny turned and gave him a kiss on the lips.

"Now it's your turn," Danny said, then went down on his knees and stuffed Mr. Valenski's swollen cock head in his mouth and sucked. He grabbed the shaft and worked on sucking the ripe knob, feeling it swell even more between his lips. Mr. Valenski held onto Danny's head and slowly eased the entire length of his rod down Danny's gullet. Spit drooled from the corners of his mouth as Danny sucked Mr. Valenski's prick, feeling the cock head swell as the shaft glided down his throat, then out, only to slip back down.

"I'm going to cum," Mr. Valenski said through clenched teeth. Danny pulled the swollen cock out of his mouth and used his spit to stroke the long, thick shaft. Mr. Valenski let out a guttural groan, then shuddered. A wave of warm cum spewed from his pulsing knob and splattered against Danny's collarbone. Mr. Valenski's body twitched as another glob of spunk spewed out of his cock. More splattered on Danny's chest in rapid succession until his neck and chest were covered in jizz.

Still on his knees and covered in creamy spunk, Danny looked up at Tim's bedroom window. It seemed as if something in the window had moved, but how could he be sure? As far as he knew, Tim was still asleep. But what if he wasn't?

"Why don't you wipe yourself off then take a dip in the pool," Mr. Valenski said.

Danny grabbed the wet towel from the chair and used it to wipe the spunk off his chest, then stepped to the edge of the pool. Mr. Valenski walked up behind Danny and wrapped his big arms around him. Danny took another peek at Tim's bedroom window.

"Tim can sleep through anything, don't be nervous," Mr. Valaenski said.

"So you've done this before," Danny said as he turned to face him.

"Never with one of Tim's friends."

Mr. Valenski had done this before without waking Tim, Danny thought as his toes curled over the edge of the pool. Danny also knew that Tim was a heavy sleeper, so Mr. Valeneski had to be right. They weren't going to be caught.

"Let's go for a swim," Danny said, then dove into the pool.

SCRATCHING THE ITCH

Lex is my roommate. He doesn't know that I'm gay, but I guess he suspects it. I could probably tell him and he'd be real cool about it, but if he wasn't I don't know what the fuck I would do. I mean, it isn't easy to find a roommate you can live with, never mind trust. Shit, Lex and I have been roommates for five years now, so why risk fucking it up over something that doesn't really concern him? We get along real well. Sometimes, when we've been drinking, he asks me when I'm going to grow some balls and get myself laid. I usually just toss him off. He takes it in stride, you know, doesn't get real pushy about it.

It's not that I don't have sex, because I do. I'll go out sometimes, telling Lex that I'm going shopping or something, when in truth I end up going to some pick up joint off the highway or to that road near the water where guys go cruising. Sometimes I make the first move, other times it's the other guy. I never take them to my place. I tell them that I live with my mother or that I have relatives over. They never question me. Usually we go to the other guy's place or split the cost of a cheap hotel room. I always have some condoms and packets of lube with me, tucked away in my jacket pocket. So it isn't like I don't get laid, you know. So what if Lex thinks I'm the only male virgin in the world. I know the truth. I mean, I would probably go insane if I never got fucked.

Lex and Ginger, his girlfriend, soon to be fiancée, are going to go to the movies. They ask if I want to go along, but I kind of feel like being alone and tell them so. I mean, I feel like jerking off. You see, Lex just plowed Ginger's pussy real good. I know because his bed kept banging against the wall as he gave her the fucking meat stick. And the whole time I've been home listening to them go at it, you know. It makes me horny knowing that he's got his cock buried in some fuck hole.

Right now Lex and Ginger are hovering around the place, getting ready to go, asking again if I'm sure I want to stay home. While they ask I'm trying to hide the fact that I've got this fucking semi-hardon begging for attention. I stand behind a kitchen chair that's waist high and tell them that I'm sure, then walk into the living room and sit on the sofa. I pretend to read a magazine just in case one of them walks in. I don't want to look like I'm sulking.

Man, she's one lucky woman to have a guy like Lex. I mean, not only is Lex a pretty good guy but his cock is fucking huge. I've seen it a number of times. He's not afraid to walk around the place naked, you know. And I guess I would miss seeing his massive cock and balls swaying back and forth if I told him about me and he ended up freaking out about rooming with a gay guy, so that's another reason why I don't tell him. I mean, sure, seeing Lex's meat hanging out all the time is a plus, but it also gets me fucking horned out too. He'll think nothing of standing in front of me and, scratching his balls while carrying on a conversation. You know, I have to find things to look at so as not to pop a boner right there in front of him. You can only look at a fucking lamp so many times!

My one big irrational fear is that some day I'm going to lose control, follow my natural instincts and go down on my hands and knees and take his fucking schlong down my throat and start sucking. In my fantasies Lex grabs my head and stuffs his cock down my throat. I can feel his cock head pressing out against the inside of my gullet as I struggle to swallow every last inch of his shaft. And when I finally get all of his cock crammed down my throat, my nose buried in his bush of curly pubic hair, he pulls it back until his ripe cock head is against my lips, leaving my throat feeling empty, then, in one swift hip movement, slams it back in. It's a great fantasy, I know, but in reality it may not be that pleasant. Lex may not take to getting sucked off by a guy too well and decide to bash me in the face. Need I say more?

Lex and Ginger say good-bye, his voice deep and looming over hers. The door closes. I hear the lock click into place, then their feet against the stairs as they make their descent. I wait a while and watch from the kitchen window as they climb into Lex's Saab. Once they're off, I walk into the living room, then the small hallway that leads to the bathroom and bedrooms. My bedroom door is on one end of the hall and his is on the opposite. The bathroom separates them. Lex's bedroom door is open, as usual. My cock is pressing against the inside of my jeans, letting me know that it wants to come out. Man, it feels real good when I rub my hand against the swell of cock, feel its massiveness beneath the jeans. It has more to grow before it gets to its fullest. I've had guys comment on the size right away, telling me that they won't let me fuck them. That's fine with me because I like a good plowing anyhow. Guys are funny, they think just because I have big dick I like to top.

I can still smell sex in Lex's bedroom. It's the smell of straight sex, but it's sex all the same. The sheets have a few stains on them. One of the stains looks like cum. He must have pulled out while he was cuming or maybe just had some spunk on his dick and rested on his stomach to talk afterwards. Who knows?

I step out of my jeans and pull off my shirt. I toss my clothes on the floor as I take them off and crawl up on the bed; press my nose against the mattress, inhale. The smell of his ass is still on the sheets. I know which side of the bed is his, and I know how his ass smells because I've wacked off on his bed before and smelled the spot where his naked ass rested. And man, that scent is his. I tickle the spot on the sheet with my tongue, pretending to be rimming his ass. I wonder if he likes that, rimming? I know I do. Man, I love to eat ass. I bet I could make him feel real good too, laying the flat of my tongue against his tight virgin fuck hole.

I'm stroking my cock, feeling it in my open palm. Stroking it slowly, picturing Lex's bare butt hovering over my face, about to make its descent. Man, he would like that. And maybe he would like to get his mouth on my fuck hole, too. Get a good taste of my pucker. I bet he would like that. I mean, straight people do that too, right? You know they do. Shit, everyone likes a good rim job. And who knows, maybe he would like to plow my ass while he's at it?

I sit on the bed, legs spread out in front of me and rub my cock against the spot where Lex sat. The sheet feels good against my shaft. It feels good knowing that I'm rubbing my cock in the spot where Lex rested. I want to cum so bad and at the same time I don't want to cum yet. I want to make this feeling last longer. I want to take my time and enjoy myself. My cock head is all ripe and swollen, my balls are rising up, moving on their own in that hairy sack of flesh. I find the cum stain on the sheets and kneel down on all fours. Sniff it. It's his cum. It's Lex's cum on the sheets. I grab my balls and pull on them, feel them stretch down. Then I spread my legs and let go of my balls. I reach between my legs and feel my pucker. Man, Lex would love my fuck hole. It's tight. All guys like a good tight hole to stick their dicks inside. And man, I bet he would love plowing my ass. He could do me real rough, too. He could just plow his cock right up my ass, pull back and ram right back in. I would take it and love it. He could ride my ass as hard as he wants and I wouldn't complain. Shit, I would be stroking my cock harder than I am now and loving every last inch of his throbbing man meat as it stroked me inside and out.

I have to stop touching my cock for fear of shooting my load. My cock is twitching, and I know that if I touch it even the slightest, if it rubs against the mattress, on that cum stain in front of me, it will explode. And man, that is not what I want. But it feels so good, the need and desire to shoot is so intense right now that I could cry. I mean, shit, I got so horny listening to Lex and Ginger go at it so loud that all I have to do is close my eyes and I can see it happen before me like I'm watching some fucking porn film. I mean, shit, there is only so much that one can take before he starts to get in the mood himself, you know.

I rub the tip of my finger inside the tight wrinkles around my asshole then bring them up to my nose. I inhale, smell my fuck hole before shoving those two fingers in my mouth, deep down my throat, getting them moist with spit, lubed up and ready to go back between my legs. And once they're there I insert them into my ass, try to spread them as wide as possible.

Come on Lex, I think, give me your cock. Come on man, fuck my ass. I insert another finger and move them in and out, feeling my ass grip those fingers as I pretend that Lex is fucking me. I pretend that my ass is gripping his cock, stretching wide to accommodate the girth of his fuck stick; pretend it's his cock moving deep within my bowels. I wish I could feel his low hanging balls slap against mine as he plows into my ass so fast that his hips slap against my butt.

I turn onto my back and lift my legs in the air; reach around my ass with both hands and spread my cheeks wide, my fingers searching for my fuck hole. When they find it I insert two fingers, one from either hand, and spread my asshole open. I imagine Lex doing this to me, getting my fuck hole ready for him to insert his shaft. I insert one more finger from either hand. Man, I want to get fucked so bad. "Fuck me," I whisper. "Come on, man, give me that big fucking cock of yours."

I raise my ass, bringing my feet up and over my head until my toes can touch the mattress. My cock bobs close to my mouth, just over my lips. I move my legs further back and open my mouth. My cock head dips inside. I can taste the pre-cum dribbling out of the tip. I pretend my cock is Lex's and start to suck on the head. It feels good. I imagine Lex telling me to suck his cock, to take it all. My fingers are still exploring my asshole, but I pretend they are Lex's fingers. My body is now his, and with that in mind I finger fuck my ass and suck on my cock head. I feel that fucking cock head get ripe and swollen once more. I know that I'm going to cum and if I cum it will be in my mouth. I wish I could taste Lex's spunk, but know that can only happen in my fantasies.

I feel my body getting ready for orgasm. At this point I wonder what Lex would do if he walked in on me. What if he stepped right through that door and saw me sucking my own cock and finger fucking my own ass? Man, what a fucking sight it would be. Would he be repulsed and walk away or intrigued and join in?

I grab hold of my shaft, keeping one hand on my ass, and give it a few strokes. I can feel my cock head about to shoot globs of hot spunk into my mouth. I am eager to swallow my own cum. My cock head throbs between my lips, cum shoots onto my tongue in repeated bursts. I quickly swallow each thick load.

When I have finished cuming in my mouth I lay flat

against the mattress, the taste of cum still prevalent. It feels good having sucked my own cock.

God, I think, what if Lex had come home early from the movie because he and Ginger had had a fight? What if he had walked in on me? I'm suddenly nervous. I get up from the bed and pick my clothes up off the floor, then walk into the bathroom and toss my clothes on the toilet; turn on the shower. I tell myself that I will never masturbate on his bed like that again, although I know that it will happen again.

I step into the shower, feel the hot spray hit my body. My balls start to hang low from the steam. I wonder what would really happen if I told Lex about me. I mean, come on, he must have an idea by now, right? And maybe, just maybe, my telling him will stop me from jerking off on his bed. You know, I could bring guys home and get laid without having to pretend I'm really doing something else. But then again, maybe not. I don't know.

I put my head under the water, close my eyes and clear my mind. I feel the water wash over me; run off my body and down the drain.

TEN THICK INCHES

It was the middle of August when Eddie the Greek hooked me into working a job with Frankie. I told him it wouldn't be a good idea, but he'd gotten me so riled up with all his talk that I couldn't say no. I was at the gym working on my pecs when he came in. He stood there while I was on my back, counting out my fifth rep of forty pounds over my head. Eddie stood there, dressed it a suit and tie and looking as cool as can be. Looking at him you'd never know he was standing in the middle of a hot gym that smelled of sweat. All you could hear was the clang of metal against metal and agonizing grunts as weights were lifted then dropped.

"It ain't a good idea, Eddie," I said, resting the weights in their place while getting a good glimpse of Eddie's thick slab of man meat beneath his slacks. The fucking guy didn't believe in wearing underwear and his schlong was always bobbing around in his slacks.

"You questioning my judgment?" Eddie said. A few heads turned on account of Eddie being so loud when he said it, and because he looked so out of place.

"No, not at all. It's just that he's got a reputation," I said.

"Don't fuck with him and he don't fuck with you," Eddie said, his voice much lower this time.

I sat up, pulled off my shirt and mopped the sweat off my brow. When I looked up, Joey was standing next to Eddie, hands on hips. The butt of Joey's gun peeked out from inside his gray suit jacket. They meant business.

"Can we talk about it?" I asked.

"Talk? Sure," Eddie said, then motioned to Joey.

The heels of Joey's shoes clicked against the cement floor as he made his way through the gym, towards the locker room. Joey came back, then followed us into the locker room. Once Eddie and I were inside, Joey stepped out and stood guard at the door.

Eddie looked around at the lockers and the wood benches, then kept his voice low and asked, "What's your gripe?"

"Everyone knows about Frankie," I said, tossing my shirt on the bench. "If he don't like you, he puts you in the line of fire."

Eddie slowly shook his head. "There 'aint no proof to that."

"How many guys get shot who work for him? More than on any other job. And easy jobs, too. And on top of that, everyone knows that the guys most likely to get hit are the ones he don't like."

"They were all goofs," Eddie said. "He'll like you, and you're good. You got nothing to worry about, so stop acting like such a little cock sucker."

"I'm not trying to give you shit, Eddie," I said, trying to keep my eyes away from his crotch. It was hard to do, especially since he was giving me that look that said he was beginning to get pissed off. And he knew what that meant for me, not that he cared.

"Then stop being such a piece of shit," Eddie said as he grabbed hold of my lower jaw and pushed me back. There was a hollow, metallic crash as my back made contact with the row of lockers behind me. His hot breath slapped against my face as he reached out and held my chest against the lockers.

"Come on, let go," I said, although his anger was making my shaft twitch.

Eddie pressed himself against my body and I felt the length of his thick slab of semi-hard man meat on my thighs. His big hand tightened on my jaw as he said, "You little fuck. Are you going to do this job or do I have to make life unpleasant?"

"I'll do it," I said, knowing he would have me whacked if I didn't.

"You bet your ass you will, you little shit," Eddie said, then stepped back. He kept his eyes on me.

I took a step to the right, holding my hands in front of me to hide my raging hardon. Then Eddie grabbed my arm and pulled me towards him. His face was inches from mine when he said, "I think you need to learn a fucking lesson. You need to find out who's boss around here, you little fuck"

Eddie pushed me to the floor, then told me to get down on my knees. He unzipped the fly to his slacks, then pulled out his massive prick. Lobbing between his legs at half mast, his thick cock waved in my direction.

"Come on, suck me off," Eddie said, grabbing my head with one hand while he used the other to slap his meat against my face.

My fingers barely touched as I took hold of his cock, then gave it a stroke. The head was a swollen, purple knob that seemed about to burst with his frothy load at any moment. Opening my mouth wide, I wrapped my lips around the bulbous head and began to suck. With each bob of my head I swallowed another inch of Eddie's meat, but that didn't seem to be enough for him. Clamping his hands on either side of my head, he held me still and slammed his prick down my throat. I gagged and swallowed as my nose was pushed into his thick bush of pubic hair and drool spilled out of the corners of my mouth.

"Come on you little cock sucker, eat it," Eddie said as he relentlessly rammed his prick in and out of my mouth, filling my gullet with his throbbing shaft.

I grabbed hold of his ass as he continued to ram his meat down my hungry throat, feeling the head swell even more than before. Then Eddie pulled his meat out of my mouth and took it in hand. He gave his shaft a few strokes, then let out a deep groan as a thick wad of hot spunk splattered against my face. The thick cream dripped down the bridge of my nose as another slapped against my forehead. The third hit my left cheek and another blew onto my chin.

"Don't you look pretty," Eddie said as he tucked his spent meat into his pants, then zipped up.

My cock was ripe for shooting as I looked up and saw Eddie walking away. All I could smell was his spunk on my face as it dripped onto the floor. My own shaft was rock hard and jerking with the need to let loose. But there was nothing I could do, since the doors were about to open to the public. Grabbing my shirt, I wiped off my face as I heard the soft patter of sneakers against tile.

"Smells like cum in here," Jerry said, his deep voice ringing out against the tiles. My cock began to go into overdrive.

"It's nothing," I said, knowing I had to say something. Jerry was the owner of the gym and he hated to think that I might have sex with anyone other than him.

"Fuck you, it's nothing. I saw that guy walk into this locker room with you," Jerry said as he stepped around the corner, his highly toned body covered in tight cotton. His hard cock was pushing out against his shorts, eager to poke out and take a stab at me.

"He has a job for me, but he didn't want to talk about it out there," I said, not wanting Jerry to think anyone but him was fucking me. I didn't want to end up paying for my gym membership. I held out my hands, hoping he wouldn't notice my boner. "Look, I'm still clothed."

Jerry shook his head as I kicked off my sneakers.

"Come on, would you just give me a break," I said.

Jerry didn't say anything as he walked up to me and shoved his big hand into my shorts. He rubbed his middle finger against my asshole, then pulled it out and gave it a whiff. With a grumble, he reached into the right pocket of his shorts and pulled out a condom. "Take them off," he said.

I pulled off my shorts, then stood against the locker in white socks and a jockstrap. I watched Jerry pull out his thin pecker and unroll the latex sheath over all seven inches. He motioned for me to turn around, so I did. We'd done this so many times that I knew exactly what Jerry wanted. I planted my hands above my head on the lockers, then separated my legs.

"That's right, just the way I like it," Jerry said as he rubbed his cock head against my eager hole. He gently poked the head into my hole, then pulled it out. Poked it in again, then eased it deep up my ass.

"Your ass is mine, do you understand that?" Jerry said as he took hold of my hair and pulled my head back.

"Yes," I said, feeling his prick glide in and out of my fuck chute.

Jerry reached around my waist and pulled my hard cock out of my jock strap. He rubbed his palm over the head, wetting it with my thick pre-cum. The head of Jerry's cock was already beginning to swell in my ass, and my own cock head felt ready to burst.

"Don't you fucking cum until I tell you to, got that," Jerry hissed. His hips slammed into my ass as his shaft began to twitch.

I clenched my teeth as I answered, "Yes."

A few guys had walked into the locker room and were standing around watching Jerry fuck me. Jerry pulled harder on my hair, then whispered, "Let these guys see what a fucking pig you are."

"Give it to him, Jerry," one of the onlookers said.

Jerry gripped my shaft and gave it a stroke as he whispered, "You want to cum so fucking bad." He pulled his cock back, then slammed it deep inside my bowels.

My knees began to give as the head of my cock begged for release. But I couldn't let my load shoot without Jerry telling me it was okay. Biting my lower lip, I felt Jerry's cock head swell and his shaft twitch. It seemed as if more men had gathered around us, watching me getting fucked.

Jerry stroked my shaft a few times as he gave my ass some quick jabs. "Come on, you fucking pig, let it fly," he said through clenched teeth.

I felt Jerry's cock head pulse up my ass, then my legs gave way and I let my own load shoot. Jerry softly groaned in my ear as my spunk covered the locker in front of me and dripped onto the floor while Jerry unloaded his frothy seed deep within my bowels.

Once he'd finished squirting his load, Jerry pulled his dick out of my ass and peeled off the condom. He didn't say anything as he proudly walked away, but I knew he thought my ass was his, and his alone.

Behind his back everyone called him Frankie Valentine because he looked so damn attractive. Dark hair, olive complexion, deep brown eyes with lashes long enough to stroke your cock from a mile away. His chest was firm, with a six pack that any guy would die for — and I am not kidding when I say die. Between his legs was a bulge that made your knees week and your asshole loosen with desire. He was also one of the toughest guys to do work for and everyone knew it.

The day I was to meet Frankie, I gripped the cool porcelain of the bathroom sink, stared into the scratchy bathroom mirror and asked myself what had come into me. Working with Frankie meant I was as good as dead. You do one thing wrong and you're a goner. Everyone knew it. His anger worked as fast as his looks. He didn't care how good you sucked his cock or if your ass was tight. Hell, his cock was so damn thick that any ass was tight enough for him. Most guys were afraid to suck his cock because they doubted it would fit down their throats. There was even a story about a guy who had suffocated to death because Frankie wouldn't take his shaft out of the guy's gullet. Nobody knew who the guy was, and there were guys out there who didn't believe the story, but I wasn't one of them. Not only that, but I had to work with him. Frankie Valentine, killer of hearts and bodies.

This might end up being my very last job, I thought. Even if I was careful, my fate depended on a man known for mastering plans that got anyone he didn't like out of the way. All I could do to save myself and come out of this alive was to work slow and keep my eyes and ears open for any sign that he might want to have me knocked off.

My first time meeting Frankie was important, so I put on my best suit and packed my favorite piece. Checking myself out in the mirror, I looked around the room, at the unmade bed and the floor littered with dirty clothes. Standing in my dumpy apartment dressed up like I had money to blow, I couldn't help but laugh at how stupid it looked.

The sun was just starting to set as I drove out across town to meet with Frankie, whose stomping ground was the old North End. The North End was like a place out of time. The streets were lined with mom and pop stores that sold meats and produce, fresh pasta and sauces, pots and pans. You name it, it was there. A slice of the Italian American lifestyle. It was a place I would like to live, but I couldn't. It wasn't my neighborhood.

I met up with Frankie at Four Corners, a bakery that had small tables in the front of the store and served coffee and ran numbers. Except for Frankie, there was one other guy sitting alone reading the paper at a table off to the side and out of sight of the door and any windows. Frankie waved me down, then took a sip from his cappuccino.

"So, you made it," Frankie said, his voice deep and rugged. His brown eyes looked straight at me, drinking in every bit of me that he could.

I put out my hand, but he didn't take it. Sitting down, I composed myself. I leaned forward and said, "So, what's this job we're about to do?"

Frankie laced his fingers together and cracked his knuckles. Gold cuff links peeked out from under his suit jacket and sparkled in the overhead lighting. He took his time looking me over, then said, "Eddie didn't tell you?"

"Nothing," I said.

Frankie took a long, slow breath. "He didn't tell you nothing?"

"Was he supposed to?"

"How about we go for a ride?"

"Sure, where to?"

"Somewhere," Frankie said. "I don't want to talk about this here."

I said it was fine, then kept my eyes open for anything suspicious. This guy cannot be trusted, I kept thinking as we walked out to his car. As nervous as I was, everything seemed to go fine. Frankie took off, driving out to Riverview Drive, which is a winding road that runs alone the Sasquahatchet River. Trees run along either side of the road, and the area is well known for lovers looking for a private place to be alone.

"Tony Montelli said you would be perfect for the job," Frankie said as he steered the car along the narrow road.

"Tony Montelli," I said, recalling the last time I had seen

that greasy lug. We'd pulled off a simple robbery job, in and out. Afterwards we'd been horsing around and started wrestling. Tony had noticed that I'd gotten a bit aroused and took full advantage of it. He'd slipped on a condom then slipped his needle dick up my ass and fucked me hard.

"You know Tony?" Frankie asked.

"Sure."

Frankie grinned, then pulled the car over to the side of the road. He turned towards me, then said, "Good. Eddie also told me you're the best guy he has for a job like this."

"What kind of job is it?"

Frankie cut the lights, then the engine. "It's something only you can pull off," he said.

"Me?"

"Do you like parties?"

"Sure," I said, wishing he would come out and tell me what the job entailed.

"I bet you look good in a tux."

"Tell me about the job."

"Are you on the team?"

"What's in it for me?"

Frankie let out a brief laugh, then very calmly said, "Fun, excitement, experience and the rest of your life."

"Well then, count me in."

"That's good," Frankie said as he tossed a piece of paper on my lap. "Meet me here tomorrow at seven o'clock in the morning."

The piece of paper he'd given me had an address not far from the bakery where I'd met him.

Needless to say, I didn't sleep well that night. What was this job Frankie was carrying out, and why was I so damn perfect for it? Not only that, but would I live to talk about it? I stalked through my apartment the whole night wondering why Eddie and Tony had told Frankie that I would be perfect for the job. There had been a few times where I'd picked up the telephone and almost dialed Eddie's number. But I couldn't do that. What if the line was tapped? I never talked about anything over the phone, and being stupid enough to do it then didn't seem logical. I wanted to live through it, even if it seemed that my chances of survival were slim.

Somehow I was able to get through the night and wake up in time to head out to the address he'd given me. As it turned out, it was to a walk-up apartment two blocks from where I'd met him the previous night. I rang the bell, then waited. The door buzzed, then I heard Frankie tell me he was on the second floor. I walked up, then saw Frankie standing in the doorway wearing nothing but a green towel around his waist, his chest was firm, with a thick tuft of hair on his upper chest. A thin line of hair cut down the middle of his muscular stomach and disappeared beneath the towel. He motioned for me to go inside, so I did.

Like myself, Frankie lived more like a con man than a mafioso. His apartment held only the bare essentials, and none of it new. Tacky paintings bought from flea markets adorned the walls, and the area rug looked more threadbare than my own, if that was possible.

"You want some coffee?" Frankie asked.

I declined, then he told me to take off my jacket and loosen my tie. With Frankie walking around with most of his beautiful body exposed, I knew it wouldn't be a good idea for me to take a seat. If I remained standing I could pretend to look around the place to distract myself from him.

"So, are you going to tell me about this job?" I asked.

"There's just one thing I need to know first," Frankie said, then dropped the towel. Frankie's thick cock dangled between his legs, the head covered by foreskin. To round out the picture, his balls hung half way down his beautiful shaft.

I stood there with my mouth open, not knowing what to

say.

"When hard, it's ten inches long and six and a half in circumference," Frankie said. "Do you think you can take it?"

My mouth watered and my asshole twitched. Unable to speak, I slowly nodded.

"Then take off your clothes and get me hard."

I did as I was told, then walked up to him and grabbed hold of his shaft, feeling it elongate and thicken in my grip. Sliding back the foreskin, I watched the plump head emerge. The more I played, the larger it became, until it was fully erect and my fingertips could no longer meet. I went down on my knees and ran my tongue along the length of Frankie's amazing prick. I began to suck on the head before inching it slowly down my hungry throat.

"Go slow, tiger, it's not your throat I care about" Frankie said.

With his shaft still in my mouth, I looked up at him.

Frankie put his hands on my head. "My dick needs to fit nice and snug up your ass in order for you to be able to take this job."

After taking his meat out of my mouth, I stood and asked what the job was.

Frankie's eyes sparkled and an evil grin spread over his face. "Someone has something of mine. A replica, if you will, in solid gold. For him it was a keepsake, something to remember me by, but I don't want him to have it. I did enough for him, he don't need anything else from me."

Frankie walked into the next room, leaving me to wonder what of his was duplicated in gold, and who had it. When he came back, he had a condom and some lubricant. I hoped he would tell me more, but all he did was walk behind me and rub lubricant on my fuck hole, sliding his fingers in and out of my ass. Not that I minded, but it would have been nice if he'd told me what I needed to know.

"Now just stand there," Frankie said as he slipped into the

condom, then pressed the head of his cock against my eager hole. I took a deep breath and relaxed, then felt my fuck hole stretch around Frankie's knob.

"Oh, that's nice," Frankie said in a whisper as he inched his prick deep inside my ass, spreading my fuck chute open to accommodate his hefty slab of meat. Once it was inside, he held it there.

I contracted my sphincter a little, then began to move away from him, but Frankie took hold of my hips to keep my ass against him. My stiff prick drooled pre-cum and began to stiffen enough to become painful.

"You like my cock up your ass, don't you," Frankie whispered.

I told him that I did.

"Do you know Victor Sintorio?"

"The crooner?"

"The very one," Frankie said, moving his hips enough to tease my hole. "If it wasn't for me, he would have never got to be as big as he is. I found him, introduced him to everyone and anyone who could make him who he is, and slipped him my meat whenever he wanted it."

"You were boyfriends?" I asked.

"No, fuck buddies. He wanted more, but I can't tie myself down to one guy. So I tell him that and he dumps me, then goes out and pays to have my cock duplicated in gold. Solid fucking gold. I want it."

Frankie pulled back further, then rammed his cock back in harder. "That little piece of shit can't duplicate my cock and think he can get away with it. That's my fucking dick, not his!"

Frankie really started fucking my hole good and hard. He pulled the entire length of his massive meat out of my bowels, then angrily forced it back in. Gulping air, I fought to keep my hole ready, feeling his fuck stick moving inside my body as the head swelled and stretched me out further.

That fucking piece of shit!" Frankie hissed, then really started slamming his prick in and out of my hole. He let out a grunt, then I felt the head of his prick pulse deep inside me as it spewed its sweet, frothy spunk up my ass.

When he'd finished cumming, his cock was still rock hard. He kept it up my ass, then reached around and took hold of my dick. "You have a tight ass," he said.

"Glad you enjoyed it," I said, hoping he wouldn't let go of my shaft, but not wanting to tell him.

"I need you to go to a party, find the duplicate of my cock, shove it up your ass, then re-join the party as if nothing happened. Can you do it?"

I swallowed, then said, "Sure."

"You have to shove all ten thick inches up your ass and be able to act as if nothing is out of the ordinary," Frankie said as he gave my cock a slow stroke up and over the head.

My legs tightened as Frankie's hand moved down my shaft, then rose back up and over my swollen knob. I wasn't sure if I was in over my head, but it didn't seem like such bad predicament with Frankie rubbing my shaft.

"Does that silence mean you can do it?" Frankie asked.

"Yes," I said.

"Good," Frankie said slow and smooth. He gave my prick two more strokes. I felt my body tense, then release a wave of hot spunk that shot out of my piss slit.

Frankie had explained the job to me before sending me home. I was to pose as Barnabas Slocum, an investment banker who had been lucky enough to score a last minute invitation. The invitation was a fake, but nobody would be able to notice, or so Frankie had promised.

Once at home, I soaked in the bathtub and contemplated what I was about to do. The job did sound fun, although having to walk around with the weight of a replica of

Frankie's thick ten inches up my ass wasn't at all appealing. I didn't have the slightest idea how to act while my ass was stuffed full of gold cock. But I had to do it, and that much I understood.

I have to admit that my dick did get hard while thinking about the job in the warm bath water. The only problem was that I could not allow myself to get a hardon while at the party. How I was going to pull it off was a mystery. All I knew was that I had to find out how before the week was out.

Frankie had said I would do fine. Once I was inside all I had to do was find a way to get to the second floor and find the gold cock without being noticed. Frankie had already found a guy who would disengage the security system for one minute. In that single minute I had to switch the actual gold cock with the replica he'd had made.

"They'll search anyone suspicious, especially if it gets found out that the piece is missing," Frankie had told me.

"A pat down, or a full body search?" I'd asked.

Frankie had looked straight into my eyes before saying, "We ain't going to find out."

He didn't know, I thought as I reached between my legs and felt the flat end of the but plug sticking out of my ass. Frankie wanted me to practice walking around with something stuck up my ass and had told me to walk around with a but plug for an hour or so every day. For me, getting caught wasn't an option, so I did as he'd suggested.

At first I would stay home and walk around the apartment with the plug up my ass, then I'd go out for a walk, to the mall, food shopping, you name it. By the time the week was up, I was as ready as I was going to be for the party.

The night of the party, I dropped by Frankie's to be inspected. The suit Frankie had bought for me was an Italian silk wool blend, no pin stripes. The tie was a solid mustard yellow, and the shirt a soft blue. I wore my best shoes, black Italian leather that I had bought the previous year and hadn't had a chance to wear.

"Good, you look perfect," Frankie said, kissing the tips of his fingers. He motioned for me to turn around.

I turned, then placed my hands on my knees and waited for him to open the hole in the seat of my slacks and insert the condom covered replica of the gold cock. The velcro for the opening between my legs spilt open, then I felt the coldness of the replica stretch my asshole. Once the object had been inserted, Frankie's fingers snaked a string down my left leg. To get the imitation out of my ass, all I had to do was pull on the string. Once it was out I had to pull fast on the string to take it off the replica, beep Sammy to disengage the alarm and make the switch.

"The guard outside the display room is one of our men, so don't worry about him," Frankie said, then winked at me. "He's very discreet."

With my ass packed full of imitation cock, I made my way to Victor Sintorio's party. Victor's small mansion took two hours to reach by car. It was situated at the edge of a cliff overlooking the ocean, where the crashing of waves mixed with the rustle of nearby trees.

After parking my car in the driveway, I walked past the two marble pillars and up the stairs leading to the double doors that were the front entrance. Two of Victor's goons, complete with black suits, stood sentry on either side of the entrance. I handed them my invitation and watched as the both of them scrutinized it before letting me enter.

The main room was filled with men in suits enjoying themselves with trivial conversation. There were a few famous faces that I was able to spot immediately, along with a few social climbers and societal fringe dwellers. There would be no problem getting lost in the crowd, but sneaking upstairs wasn't going to be such an easy task.

With my head held high and my ass cheeks clenched, I walked into the crowd. A handsome young man in a tuxedo held out a silver tray filled with glasses of wine. I accepted a glass, then continued to make my way through the crowd. I was immediately assaulted by Aaron Teller, the television producer who had begun his career in the seventies. His short gray hair was thick, well styled, and made him appear somewhat respectable. I introduced myself as Barnabas Slocum, then told him I was an investment banker.

"I thought you were an actor," Aaron said, his sparkling blue eyes working hard to enchant.

"Unfortunately not," I said with a smile. "But I'm sure this would be the place if I were."

"Not the perfect place, but it wouldn't hurt," Aaron said. "After all, there are so many places two men could go to talk privately about finding work."

"I'm afraid I wouldn't know, having never taken a tour of the house."

Aaron gleefully took the bait and offered to show me around. Slipping his arm around my waist, he asked which floor I would like to see first. I told him the second would seem the best place to start, since it was away from everything.

"Well then, that is where we will begin," Aaron said as he led me through the crowd. I followed Aaron to the rear of the house, where I was able to hand my wine glass over to one of the boys working the event.

"It's an old servants' staircase," Aaron said as we made our way upstairs.

The second floor hall was spacious, with hard wood floors and a deep blue runner that muffled our steps. I already knew the layout from the floor plans Frankie had shown me. The room where the gold shaft was displayed was through the last door on the left.

"You have to see the guest room," Aaron said, his hand

wandering from my lower back to the outward curve of my ass.

I turned towards him and grinned. He escorted me into the guest room, then closed the door. Without looking around, I grabbed Aaron's crotch and gave it a squeeze. I looked into Aaron's beautiful blue eyes, then gave him a gentle kiss on the lips.

Aaron's hands slid onto my ass as he said, "I would love to fuck you."

My hole clenched at the thought of having Aaron shove his prick into my ass, only to have its contents pushed even further inside my body. "Not now," I said, giving Aaron's already stiff meat another squeeze.

I went down on my knees and unzipped his fly. Aaron let out a soft, pleasurable moan as I reached inside and pulled out his thick, uncut cock. I gave the shaft a stroke, watched as the cock head peeked out of the extra skin, then wrapped my lips around the purple knob. The flat end of the reproduction of the gold shaft poked against my sphincter, threatening to pop out, so I clenched my asshole tight as I sucked on the head of Aaron's dick.

"That feels so good," Aaron said softly as he ran his fingers through my hair.

I slid the remaining six inches down my throat, then pulled back and swallowed the length of his shaft once more. With my eyes closed, I concentrated on keeping my fuck hole tight while attempting to give Aaron the best blow job he'd ever received. So far it seemed to be working.

Grabbing his shaft, I worked the head in my mouth, sucking long and hard on it. Aaron's soft moans continued as the head of his prick plumped up even more. Finally he was close, and his breathing sounded labored and heavy. He let out a deep groan as I pulled his cock out of my mouth and began stroking it.

"Shit, I'm going to cum," Aaron said through clenched

teeth.

Still on my knees, I moved back and watched as Aaron sprayed his jizz on the floor, covering it with pearls of white.

Aaron finished cumming, then looked down at the floor. His eyes widened as he said, “Oh my, I seem to have made a mess on the floor. There should be a towel in the bathroom. I’ll get it and clean this up.”

“No, you go downstairs and let me clean it up,” I said, eager to get rid of him and complete the job.

“Don’t you want a little reciprocation?”

“Later, after the party? The two of us, naked.”

“You bad boy,” Aaron said with a devilish grin before opening the door and walking off.

I quickly grabbed a towel then wiped the cum off the floor before slipping on a pair of latex gloves. After that I made my way down the hall and into the room where the gold cock was proudly displayed. As Frankie had said, one of his men was standing sentry at the entrance. He winked, then stood outside while I went to work.

There it was, the gold cock, standing up on a marble pedestal. An overhead light shone down on it, making the bright gold sparkle and shine in the light.

Squatting down, I opened the hole in my slacks then found the string and gave it a gentle tug. My asshole popped open and out slid the replica covered in its latex sheath. Before my hole had time to close back up, I yanked the string off, then peeled the condom off and disposed of it. I gave the replica a quick shine on my slacks. The transmitter for the guy who would fix the security system was in my pocket. I hit the button and trusted he’d done his job.

I took a deep breath, then reached out and grabbed the gold cock and made the switch. Once again I squatted, then positioned the gold shaft against my pucker. My ass ring had already begun to close up and I felt it grip the shaft as it eased back up my ass. Biting my lip, I tried not to make a sound as

I quickly sat on it, feeling it fill my bowels. Reaching between my legs, I made sure the end wasn't sticking out and that my hole was as closed as it was going to get.

After standing up, I put the latex gloves into the disposal bag, closed it up and put it inside my coat pocket. Frankie's man nodded as I passed him, then quickly kept to the carpet as I made my way back towards the rear staircase. Voices echoed from the front staircase as I began to make my descent. Just in time, I thought as I eased my way back to the first floor.

"Oh good, you made it," Aaron said as I emerged from the staircase. His eyes grew wide. "Victor is rounding everyone up to view the gold cock?"

"I took a peek while I was up," I said.

"And how was it?"

"Amazing, you really have to see it," I said, hoping Aaron wouldn't ask me to view it again. I wasn't sure how long the fake cock would fool Victor.

"I guess it pays to be sneaky," Aaron said, slipping his hand inside his jacket pocket. He pulled out a business card and handed it to me.

I looked down at the card, then said, "It doesn't have your home phone number, only your e-mail address."

"I don't give that out to just anyone."

"I'm not just anyone."

"Prove it," he said, then walked away.

Shocked and aroused, I watched Aaron leave the room to unknowingly view a replica of the original. It wasn't long before I made my exit, trying to look as casual as possible. The gold cock was buried up my ass, causing slight discomfort. Still, I walked tall and steady. At the door, the goons in black turned towards me.

"Wait," the goon on the left said, then stepped up to me and slid hands inside my jacket and down my torso.

"Is something the matter?" I asked, trying not to clench my

ass cheeks too hard. I didn't want to do anything to make him go any further than my legs.

"Preliminary," he said, then went down on his knees and slid his hands down my pant legs. His face was close to my crotch, and I caught him peeking at the bulge of my semi-hard cock.

"Have you seen it?" I asked.

He looked up at me and blushed.

"The statue."

He stood, then said, "Not yet. Maybe when everyone is gone."

"I'm sure," I said, then walked back to my car.

I drove to Frankie's place, taking side roads while keeping a close eye in the rear view mirror. It didn't seem as if anybody was following me, but I didn't want to risk it. With every bump the gold cock seemed to burry itself deeper up my ass, making me wonder if it would ever come out.

When I arrived at Frankie's place, he was ready for me. He looked dressed as if he was ready to head out for a night on the town, despite the fact that he wasn't wearing a tie. I pulled off the suit jacket and tossed it on the sofa, then undid the tie and did the same with that.

"All you need to do is take off the slacks and bend over," Frankie said.

Slowly, I unbuckled my belt as Frankie glared at me. Without saying a word, I unbuttoned the top of the slacks, then grabbed hold of the small metal tab on the zipper.

"This isn't a fucking strip show," Frankie said, reaching out and yanking the zipper down. He reached into my pants and took hold of my hard cock. He gave it a tug, then took his hand off it and pulled my pants down to my ankles.

The look in his eyes told me not to defy him any further, so I went down on my knees. Frankie knelt beside me, then slipped his index finger up my ass, feeling the flat end of the gold cock. He inserted four fingers up my ass, then spread my hole open.

"Give it a little push," he said.

I pushed, feeling the gold cock slowly slide down my fuck chute, rubbing against my prostate. My dick twitched as a soft moan escaped my lips. The gold cock seemed to glide out further on its own, then it slid in a little and out again.

"You like it, you fucking pig," Frankie said.

"I'd rather have the real thing," I said, keeping my hole relaxed while Frankie slipped the entire ten thick inches out of my hole.

"I'd rather fuck you when your hole is tighter," Frankie said, giving my ass a slap.

Sitting on the floor, I watched as Frankie held up the gold cock and examined it. For the first time I was able to get a good look at the item I'd just stolen. Frankie unzipped his slacks, then lugged out his semi-hard cock. He gave it a stroke, then held the replica of his cock next to it. The likeness was amazing. Inch for inch they were the same.

"How would you like to suck on the real thing?" Frankie said as he stood up.

Without saying a word, I was down on my knees with Frankie's huge meat stuffed down my throat. I sucked his shaft and he told me how good it felt and how he wanted to spray his load all over my pretty face. He wanted to see his thick cum dripping down my face and rub it in with his shaft.

Frankie drove me wild with that dirty talk. His right hand grabbed hold of a lock of my hair and steadied my face while his prick slammed in and out of my mouth. Spit drooled out of the corners of my mouth while I fought to keep my throat open.

I waited until Frankie sprayed my face with his thick load before I reached down and touched my aching cock. He rubbed his meat against my face, rubbing his seed into my skin while I gave my prick a few strokes.

My body twitched as the first wave of spunk shot out of

my piss slit. Frankie called me a little slut as I came on his floor in the longest orgasm I'd ever had.

It took a few days for the forgery to be found out. And although the news never hit the papers, I'd heard about it through my sources at the police station. Despite the fact that I couldn't call him, Aaron's business card was sitting on my bureau at home. Every morning I'd wake up and look at it, then remind myself to throw it away. But I couldn't. There was something about the guy that I liked. Maybe it was his eyes, or the promise of a little sexual reciprocation? I didn't know, nor could I risk finding out. Nobody at the party knew who I was, and the last thing I needed to do was risk getting caught. The job I'd done for Frankie was finished, I needed to forget about that night and get on with my life.

It had been a week before I'd been able to get back to the gym. The last thing I needed was for Jerry to find out that something other than his prick had been fucking me. At the gym everything had seemed fine. The mindless lifting of weights, counting out reps, working my body just enough to stay in shape was a relief. Slowly I'd begun to forget about Frankie and the gold cock. Then one day, after I'd stripped and closed my gym locker, someone walked up to me and said, "Are you up for another job?"

It was Frankie.

BEAT THE DRUM

It was the chanting that drove me out of my apartment. You see, I was living in one of those old fashion U shaped buildings popular in the thirties and forties. My apartment was in the right, inside corner next to a woman who chanted every evening at six o'clock. It was a religious thing for her, the chanting. She believed it helped release whatever was keeping her from moving ahead with her life. I believed it was keeping me from being sane.

Her chanting had never really bothered me before, but, you know, that day was a real scorcher, mid August, hot and muggy. Despite the fact that there wasn't a breeze to be felt for miles, I had all my windows open hoping to get some cross ventilation. All I ended up getting was her repetitive chanting of "I am nothing. I am nothing. I am nothing." It was like being on hold and forced to listen to a Gregorian Chant put to Muzak.

Now, I have a high tolerance level, but in that sweltering heat my tolerance was growing thin. I had to get away from her constant droning before I went completely mad. I'd been pacing since she'd begun her endless cycle of monotone nonsense, so I thought it would be a good time to arrange my pots and pans, but her voice still went on. It was clearly obvious that masturbation was not going to be an option, so I decided to step out for a walk.

Outside wasn't any different from inside. Moisture hung in the air like clothes on a line. Yes, another fucking New England summer. My shorts were real loose and my balls kept sticking to my thighs. I walked, checking out people strolling along the street, on their way home or wherever. Then I saw this guy sitting on the front steps of this old gray Victorian house. The ornate double doors had a row of doorbells running along the right side, which was typical for houses that had been converted to apartments. The guy was sitting back, reclining against the wrought iron banister, wearing nothing but a pair of thin running shorts that showed off the bulge of cock and balls hanging inside. He looked kind of laid back, almost as if he was actually leaning against a palm tree and not the banister of some old house. And his deep brown skin tone, dark wavy hair, emerald green eyes and full lips helped the tropical image he'd conjured.

The guy ran his long, thick fingers through his hair, then down his neck and across his firm chest. He looked hot in every sense of the word. Looking straight at me, he asked, "What's up?"

"Just taking a stroll," I said, trying not to appear too cruisy. I mean, this guy didn't really come off as gay or anything, just sexy.

"It wouldn't be so bad if it wasn't so humid," he said, picking up a pack of clove cigarettes from behind him. He pulled one out along with a book of matches. I watched the match flame dance at the end of the cigarette as he lit it. He blew the match out in a stream of scented smoke, then tossed it onto the sidewalk.

"Every now and again I feel the need for one of these," he

said, holding up the clove cigarette. "They dip the end in honey so the taste stays with you." He laughed as if to himself. "Like Ambrosia."

"But they can't be that good for you," I said.

The guy shrugged, took another drag. Smoke trailed behind his words as he said, "I don't smoke that much."

The subtle scent of burning cloves filled the air with its intoxicating scent, making the heat almost bearable. All I wanted to do was prolong my time with this guy, so I lamely said, "At least it smells better than regular cigarettes."

The guy grinned and spread his legs, resting his right foot one step below the other. His cock pushed out against the thin material of his shorts, long and thick. "Take a seat if you want," he said. "As long as you have time to spare."

"I'm in no rush," I said, feeling my cock twitch. I rubbed my thighs, then sat next to him. "I still can't believe how humid it is."

"Yeah," he said, "so many things just cling to the air as if they're stuck for some reason." He looked down, holding the cigarette between his legs, then leaned back on his elbows. He extended his legs even further and flexed his toes. His cock was stretched out along his thigh, reaching towards the very bottom of his shorts.

"It makes people cranky," I said, trying not to look at his bulging cock. My own dick was already semi-hard. I tried not to move so it wouldn't rub against the inside of my shorts.

"This weather gets me horny, you know. There's just something about the heat and all that does it to me. Maybe it's the way your clothes just cling to your body, or that subtle human scent that guys sometimes give off in the heat," he said, then flicked the cigarette butt into the street. He reached out and touched my forearm, then gently ran his fingers down to my hand. He turned my hand around, then traced a line on my palm.

Unable to say a word, I looked up at him and met his

haunting gaze. His eyes seemed to draw me into him, then I felt his lips against mine and the sweet taste of honey as my mouth opened to greet his tongue. Slowly, I pulled back and tried to compose myself.

"Shall we go upstairs?" he asked.

"Sure," I said, then stood up and followed him inside.

We went up a creaky set of stairs, to the third floor, where he stopped in front of the only door on that landing. He opened the door, then we walked inside a dimly lit room sparsely furnished with an old worn sofa and love seat that seemed as if they'd been placed at the first available space and forgotten. The Oriental rug was a faded design of vines, leaves and flowers. The rug was so thin that the hard wood floor was visible in some areas. Against the wall to my right were two doors, both of which were closed.

"My roommate isn't home. If he does come home, he might start playing the drums. I hope you don't mind," he said, then walked up to the door on the left and opened it.

The room was pitch black, so I waited for him to turn on a light before entering. He lit a pillar candle set on the floor to the right of a futon mattress, casting the room in a yellow, flickering glow. I scanned the room in search of a hutch, high boy or dresser, but found none. Across from me, on the far wall, was an open window void of curtains. When I looked back at the man who had brought me into his apartment, he was standing at the foot of the bed, naked. His big, thick shaft was rock hard and his balls hung low in their loose sack of flesh. He slowly extended his long arms, then said softly, "Come, join me."

I undressed, leaving my clothes in a pile on the floor, then stepped up to him. He wrapped his arms around me, holding me close. Our stiff shafts rubbed one against the other as we kissed long and deep. I kissed his neck, tasting the salt of his skin, taking in the odor of cloves and sweat. My lips made their way to his chest, then his arm pit. The musky scent of his body drove me wild with lust, and I ran my tongue along the outer edge of his pit as he let out soft moans of approval.

My hands gently slid down his back as I lowered myself onto my knees, gliding my lips and tongue down his chest and stomach. My palms caressed the firm curves of his ass as my fingers explored the warm crack where the two mounds met. After sucking his balls into my mouth, I felt them against my tongue, then slowly set them free one at a time.

The man pulled his fingers through my hair as I grabbed his thick rod, feeling its heavy weight in my grip. I looked at it, then ran my tongue along the outer edge of the knob. Slowly, I began stroking it. I breathed in the scent of his balls, then began licking around his fleshy sack. He softly sighed his approvals as I worked his prick until a thin stream of pre-cum drooled out of the tip.

The man let out a long sigh, then the soft, hollow drum beat started.

Each beat of the drum was evenly spaced from the next in a constant, slow, hypnotic rhythm. The man brought his right hand down under my chin, then asked me to stand. When I did as he'd instructed, we kissed. As we kissed, his hands roamed my body while his mouth opened to my tongue. Without taking his lips from mine, he slowly lowered us onto the futon mattress on the floor.

When our lips parted, his body was on top of mine, warm and smooth. His hot breath rushed past my right ear in time with the slow drum beats as his heavy cock rubbed against my flesh. Then he moved down and kissed my left nipple. He tickled it with the tip of his tongue, then gently sawed it between his teeth as he pinched the other one. The more he worked my nipples, the heavier my breathing became. Finally, I let out a gasp, feeling the threshold of pleasure and pain. He stopped what he was doing and looked up at me, his green eyes aglow in the dim light.

He reached down and played with my balls as he lowered

himself further down my body. He stuck his tongue in my navel, then ran the tip out and through my wiry bush of pubic hair. My stiff cock brushed against his smooth face as he grabbed my balls and tugged on them. My body tightened and I let out a moan. Then I felt his tongue drift over the length of my shaft. When he reached the tip, he gave it a gentle kiss and let his lips linger at the head for a minute.

My body tightened once more as he gave my nuts a gentle tug. I heard him breathing and felt his breath against my shaft. Then he let go of my balls and started licking and sucking them as his hands gripped my inner thighs. His thumbs drifted between my legs, pressing against the skin between my balls and asshole. I raised my legs and felt his thumbs move closer to my pucker. He whispered something, then pressed his lips against my fuck hole and gave it a kiss.

Opening my eyes, I saw the room aglow in flickering yellow. The man placed his hands on the back of my thighs and pushed them towards me, lifting my ass higher to expose my tight fuck hole. He licked the thin cord of flesh that ran from my balls to my ass, then pressed the whole of his tongue against it. Unable to hold back, I let out a soft moan and pushed my ass towards his face.

The drum beat quickened.

The man slid his tongue up my hole as he pressed his lips against it. I raised my legs higher, heard the drum beat quicken, then felt more of his tongue glide up my ass. His tongue slid out, then plunged back inside me, deeper than it had gone before. Then I felt his thumbs slide inside my ass, stretching my sphincter as his tongue continued to probe my hole. My cock throbbed, eager to shoot the load of hot spunk that filled it. His tongue continued to probe my fuck chute as his thumbs continued to stretch open my ass. The pleasure was intense, and my cock began to twitch. A deep, guttural groan rose up from my chest. The drum beat became even faster.

I went to grab hold of my prick, but my right hand could not move. I tried again, but felt it tug away, as if being bound to the right hand corner of the mattress. The same happened when I tried to touch myself with my left hand. Then I felt something slide up my ass that did not feel like a tongue or a finger. Panicked, I raised my head and saw the guy still on all fours between my legs. It was his tongue licking my hole, fucking me with long, penetrating jabs that quickly rushed past my sphincter as his fingers stretching me open even further. Unable to handle the pleasure, my back arched.

The sound of rapid drum beats filled the room. Feeling hot spunk fill my shaft as the man's tongue continued to fuck my ass, rubbing against my prostate, driving me wild with lust. I closed my eyes and fought the urge to cum. There was no way I was going to allow a stranger to have total control over my body.

A breeze from the open window rushed past me, cooling my flesh. And somewhere, off in the distance, I could hear the soft chanting in time with the drum beats. Nothing, nothing, nothing, nothing, nothing, nothing.

The guy had stopped eating my ass and let my legs fall back to the mattress. Keeping my eyes closed, I felt his warm body straddle my legs. I looked up at him; saw his green eyes glowing in the flickering yellow light of the room. Still, the soft chanting and heavy drum beat continued. The man's cock rose high between his legs, rising past his navel. He straddled my shaft so it was between his balls and thighs, then began to move his hips back and forth with the rhythm of the drum.

With my arms bound to the corners of the mattress, all I could do was watch as he straddled me, rubbing his inner thigh against my hard cock, driving me wild with lust. His lips began to move as if he was chanting with the people in the distance. Nothing. Nothing. Nothing.

Cum built in my prick, swelling the head as he continued to ride my shaft. As much as I wanted to shoot my load, I fought to hold back. It was as if we were fighting for control of my orgasm. All I could feel was the ecstacy of sex and none of the pleasure. My back arched, my toes curled, my breathing was heavy. I let out a soft moan. I needed to cum.

"Set me free," the man said, his voice filling the room as he continued to glide his hips over my shaft, yellow light flickering over his deep brown skin. Then he held out his arms and looked up. His cock began to twitch, then I felt it, the first wave of cum about to shoot from my prick. It seemed as if every muscle in my body tightened, and I let out deep, guttural groan. Hot, creamy jizz shot out of my piss slit and slapped against my neck and chin. The next shot streamed out, landing on my chest. My back arched once more, then another shot burst free, landing on my pectorals, then another. Then finally the orgiastic bursts slowed, as did the drum beats, until both were spent.

My arms were free, but I was too exhausted to move. Beside the mattress, the flame on the candle flickered once, then died. The room was dark, and I was alone. Closing my eyes, I felt exhaustion fill my body and soothe me to sleep.

The next day I woke up and looked around. Nothing had changed. The room contained the same old furniture and smelled of dust and age. The candle beside the mattress was now unlit. A cool breeze rushed through the open window, so I walked up to it. Outside, the sun was shining and there were small puddles on the sidewalk. The rain had cooled everything down, I thought.

My clothes were in a heap on the floor, just where I had left them. But there was no sign of the man who had brought me there. After getting dressed, I called out, "Hello."

There was no answer, so I walked into the living room. The door to the guy's roommate's bedroom was open a crack. I tapped on the door. When there was no response, I walked inside. Except for a tall bongo drum in the very center, the room was empty. Dried red beans were scattered across the floor as if spilled and abandoned. I walked back into the living room and said hello once again. Still, no answer.

There was nothing else to do, so I left. Perhaps the man would be sitting out on the steps, I thought. He wasn't there either. People casually strolled along the sidewalk and cars drove by. It was just like any other day.

After stepping down to the sidewalk, I turned and looked up at the old house. Two of the windows on the first floor were boarded up and there was an abandoned building sign on the front door. I couldn't remember seeing those things the previous night, although they could have been there. I had been too busy concentrating on the sexy, dark skinned man sitting on the steps. I'd spent the night with that guy and didn't know who he was or where he went. A cool breeze drifted past me and I looked up at the clear blue sky. Somehow I knew I would never see him again.

BODIES IN MOTION

Sam's cock stiffened in his tight jeans as he listened to the melodic rhapsody of the four boys that composed the group Bodies in Motion. At the age of thirty he knew he was too old to be a groupie, but had bought the poster for their new album, *Because We Can*, anyhow. The poster was unrolled on the living room floor, the four band members staring up at him. They look so tough, but sound so pretty, Sam thought as he gazed down at them. All four wore matching leather biker jackets and t-shirts, and not single one was smiling. Although each band member was over eighteen, only one of the four had facial hair, Ted. Ted's dark hair was cut military short, and looked as if it was going to show signs of receding in a year or two. Ted was the kind of boy men like to put over their knee and give a good spanking. To Ted's right was baby-faced Ed, whose thin lips and dark eyes made him look mysterious despite his typical, combed-to-the-side, conservative haircut. Sam could see himself rubbing his naked body against Ed and kissing his pretty face for hours. Justin was to Ted's left. Justin had full lips that longed to suck cock. His deep brown hair was short and well groomed. To Justin's left was Kurt, the boy next door type. There was nothing special about Kurt's appearance, but he seemed to be the boy parents trusted but shouldn't. The kind of kid parents would never suspect of seducing their sons. And although he wasn't bad looking, there was nothing that drew the eye towards him.

Sam grabbed his crotch again, feeling his thick eight inches stretch out, rubbing against the inside of his jeans. Behind him the boys sang a sweetly gentle love song, their melodic voices filling the room. Grabbing the bottom of his olive green t-shirt, Sam pulled it up, over his head and let it fall on the thick nap of the beige wall to wall carpet. He kicked off his boat shoes, then felt the carpet beneath his feet. He imagined the boys running their hands over his smooth chest, down his tight stomach, over his well defined pecs. Falling onto his knees, Sam stuffed the three fingers of his left hand down his throat. If only the boys would let him suck their cocks. He wanted to feel them pump their meat in and out of his face, have their balls slap against his chin. They would all stand around him and stroke their meat while waiting for him to service them one by one.

Sam pulled on the waist of his jeans, then heard the ripple of buttons becoming undone. He dipped his hand into his jeans, then lobbed out his thick cock and heavy balls. The fingers that were down his throat were covered with spit as he slipped them out of his mouth. Shoving the moist fingers into the back of his jeans, he rubbed his tight pucker, then pushed two of the fingers inside the hole. Oh man, Sam thought, if only they would fuck my ass. Maybe he could have Ed fuck his ass while Justin slipped his rod in and out of his mouth. The other two would watch, maybe even egg their band members on, telling them to fuck him good and hard. The thought was enough to make Sam's shaft twitch for joy.

Sam pulled his fingers out of his ass, then rolled onto his

back. His cock was rock hard, the head swollen and ready to burst. Holding his fingers under his nose, he inhaled the ripe scent of his fuck hole, then stuffed them in his mouth. Sam imagined Justin squatting over his face as he slid his tongue over the tight wrinkle of his ass. The others would stand over him, slowly stroking their dicks.

Sam grabbed hold of his stiff prick and slipped his hand up and down the shaft with long, slow strokes. He imagined the other band members standing over him, doing the same with their meat. He wanted to hear them softly moan as they shot their loads on him. He wanted to feel their hot spunk splatter against his chest, on his neck and his face. Sam's legs tightened, his neck arched back, then he let out a groan. The first spurt of hot cum spewed out of his piss slit and splattered against his stomach. The next wave of spunk shot out, then another glob burst free.

Sam wore a pair of button fly jeans and a Bodies in Motion t-shirt as he gripped the handle of the shopping carriage and searched through the aisles of the grocery store for food. He was eyeing a bunch of bananas when he heard the title song from Bodies in Motion's new CD. Rubbing his hand over the picture of the four boys on his t-shirt, he began humming along with the tune as he searched the bananas for the ripest bunch. Gliding his fingers along the yellow fruit, feeling the smooth skin, he found a good bunch then placed it in the metal carriage. The boys sounded so beautiful, and the tune was so catchy that Sam found his fingers slowly tapping on the grip of the carriage as he wheeled it through the produce department.

The zucchini were nice and green, he thought as he parked his carriage next to them and reached out to feel the long, thick vegetable. The deep, melodic refrain came through the speakers. "We only do it because we can," Sam softly sang along as he gripped the ripe zucchini. With his eyes closed, he could see the handsome members of the boy band looking up at him as they slowly stroked their engorged cocks and softly sang to him. What he wouldn't do to see them in person.

Sam began to wheel the carriage down the aisle once more when he realized that his cock was stiff and rubbing against the inside of his jeans. Afraid that he might cum if he continued to walk, he stayed put next to the zucchini. He already had one of the green tubular vegetables in his carriage, but pretended to be interested in picking another. The song was ending. He hoped his prick would go down. When it didn't, he went into the frozen food section, opened the glass door and stood close to the frozen deserts until his erection went down.

Once the engine started, the radio began to play the final notes of the second hit from the Bodies in Motion CD. Sam sat back and listened, then the disc jockey came on trying to sound cool and hip, although Sam thought the guy sounded like a dweeb.

"That was *Be Mine*, the latest hit from Bodies in Motion," the disc jockey said. "Bodies in Motion will be coming to Providence next week, and I have tickets and back stage passes to give to caller three."

Sam almost jumped out of his seat as he lunged for the glove compartment and pulled out his cell phone. He pushed the speed dial button he'd programmed for the radio station, then waited. It was busy. He hit redial. Busy. Redial again. Waited. It rang! His cock began to shift in his pants as he waited for someone to pick up. There was the click, then the disc jockey's voice.

"Am I number three?" Sam asked as he lunged at the car radio and turned down the volume.

"Yes you are," the DJ said.

"You're kidding!" Sam had to try not to scream. "I can't believe it! Back stage passes!"

"That's right, tickets to the show and backstage passes for two."

Sam bounced in his seat a few times as he tried to calm himself down.

"Do you know who you're going to bring?" the DJ asked.

"Not yet," Sam said. "I can't believe it. I'm going to meet them! They're my favorite band."

"I can tell," the DJ said. "Why don't you hold on and we'll get you set up with the tickets."

Sam waited, then was passed on to another guy who took down his name, phone number and address. Sam had a raging boner by the time he was finished. Grabbing the bulge of hard cock between his legs, Sam began to rub. He sat back, closed his eyes and imagined walking into the back stage dressing room and seeing all four of the band members standing around in the their underwear. They'd stop humming the tune they'd been practicing, then look at him and smile. They'd ask him inside, close the door behind him. He'd be able to touch them, talk to them. He'd see what they were really like.

Sam took in a sharp breath as he felt his legs tighten. His head tilted back and he let out a soft moan. Between his legs, his cock twitched once more as the head of his cock pulsed out another shot of spunk.

Sam snapped back to reality, looked down at the wet cum stain that covered his left thigh, then looked out at the parking lot. Everybody was going about their business, unaware that he'd just won tickets and back stage passes to Bodies in Motion and had an orgasm. He turned the key in the ignition, then pressed his foot on the gas peddle. Quickly, he drove out of the parking lot of the grocery store.

—

By the time Sam got home from the grocery store his cock was rock hard again, and wasn't about to go down any time soon. Damn that radio station for playing another song by Bodies in Motion, Sam thought as he peeled off his stained jeans, then his underwear. He grabbed his stiff cock as he walked into the bathroom to toss his soiled clothes in the hamper. He could jerk off again, but he was still exited about having won tickets and backstage passes and needed to tell someone. He made his way back into the living room and went to the telephone.

The light on the answering machine indicated that he had a message. He hit play and waited. It was Erik, whose slight Latino accent gave his deep voice just what it needed to make Sam's cock twitch. Erik asked if he wanted to get together with him. Sam grinned, then grabbed the telephone. He knew that Erik only called for one reason, and that was to get laid. He called Erik back and told him to come on over.

It took no time at all for Erik to arrive once Sam got off the phone with him. Sam opened the door and there was Erik, standing with his arms crossed as if he'd had to wait far longer than he'd wanted. Sam looked into Erik's deep brown eyes, then asked him inside.

"Love your t-shirt," Erik said as he brushed past him. Erik unbuttoned his green plaid shirt, exposing his smooth, firm chest.

Sam couldn't help but notice how Erik's brown skin played beautifully with his steel blue carpenter pants. Shifting his eyesight back towards Erik's face, he said, "You look great."

Erik's eyes washed seductively over Sam's torso. "I would like to see you naked."

"Not yet," Sam said as he ran his open palm over Erik's smooth body. "I have something to ask you."

"Do you really?" Erik said, slipping his hands under Sam's Bodies in Motion t-shirt and rubbing his thumbs around

Sam's aureolas. "Can it wait?" Erik gently bit Sam's neck, then pressed his stiff cock against Sam's thigh. "I am so horny."

Sam stepped away from Erik before things went too far and he wouldn't have time to ask. Erik looked at him, his eyes sad with rejection.

"I want to take you to see Bodies in Motion with me," Sam said.

Erik's eyes lit up as he crossed his arms. "What does this mean? Is it a date?"

"Well, not really," Sam said, being careful not to stumble over his words. "You're the only guy I know who might want to go with me."

"Oh, I see, then," Erik said. "You want me to dish out money to go to a concert so you won't be alone in a crowd of giggling teenagers."

"You don't have to pay."

"I have money and a job, Samuel." Erik said indignantly.

"No, you don't have to pay. I won the tickets."

Erik looked suspicious. "You won them?"

"Tickets and backstage passes."

"And you want to take me?"

"I would like you to go with me, yes," Sam said.

"Backstage, too?"

"Yes."

Erik grinned, then reached out and slipped his hands under Sam's t-shirt. He pulled Sam towards him, then gently kissed his lips. "Well now, that changes everything," he said.

"Does it?" Sam asked, unzipping Erik's pants and dipping his right hand inside. He took hold of Erik's big, thick slab of cock and pulled it out. The warmth and stiffness of it felt so good in his grip.

"It does," Erik said softly.

Sam went down on his knees, then rubbed Erik's cock against his face. He licked the shaft, then wrapped his lips around the purple knob and sucked on it. Erik sighed and moaned as Sam slowly slid the entire length of Erik's prick down his hungry throat, feeling the girth fill his gullet.

"That feels so good," Erik said as he held Sam's head still and began to pump his love muscle in and out of his face. Erik's big balls slapped against Sam's chin with every inward thrust, and the head of his cock soon became ripe with spunk.

"Oh fuck," Erik hissed, then pulled his prick out of Sam's mouth and began stroking it. He let out another grunt, then his body jerked. A spray of hot cum shot out of his piss slit and landed on the bridge of Sam's nose. Erik let out another grunt as another thick glob of fuck juice slapped against Sam's left cheek. The third hit Sam's chin and dripped onto the floor.

When he'd finished cumming, Erik slid down on his knees and kissed Sam once more. "I am so glad you asked me to go to the concert with you," he said, his hands reaching between Sam's legs and unzipping his fly. He licked the cum off Sam's chin, then went down and began to suck his cock.

Both Sam and Erik were the oldest people at the concert. Sam had worn his tightest cotton pullover, which accented every ripple of muscle in his upper torso, and a pair of beige chinos. Most of the crowd were screaming kids who were eagerly waiting for Bodies in Motion to come on while the opening band played. Only three rows away from the stage, Sam and Erik also waited through the ongoing songs from the band on the stage. The band was Liquid Video, and although Sam had an idea of who they were, Erik had never heard of them.

Liquid Video had sung their final song, then went off stage to mild applause. Erik sat there and waited for Bodies in Motion to come on stage. He watched as the stage was being set up and listened to the whisperings of boys also waiting to see and hear their favorite band perform live. At one point Erik had mentioned that he thought they were the oldest people there. Sam didn't want to hear that, nor did he care. He was about to see Bodies in Motion live, and his dick was already beginning to respond to the event.

Finally the lights went dark, the music to their song, *Just What I Want,* swelled and the crowd began to scream. Sam shot up to his feet, clapping and screaming. The lights blared, then lowered. Sam and everyone around him screamed once more. Then he saw Bodies in Motion on stage. Dressed in simple street clothes that were tight enough to show off their toned physiques, they danced and sang. Sam danced in place with them and sang along.

Throughout the concert Sam felt his hardon rubbing against the inside of his jeans. The thin metal chain around his neck with the backstage pass on it was a constant reminder that he and Erik were going to meet the band. During the ballad, *Thinking of You*, Erik gently rubbed Sam's ass. Sam slid the back of his hand against Erik's stiff prick, then leaned against his left shoulder.

"Don't get all romantic on me," Sam said.

Erik chuckled. "I'm thinking of fucking your ass."

Sam looked up at the stage and wondered if perhaps they could entice the boys to join them. If they could, then that would be a night they would not forget.

When the concert was finished, Sam and Erik waited for the crowd to thin a little before making their way to the aisle. They walked towards the stage, where they were greeted by a tall, rugged security officer who pointed out how to get to the dressing room once they showed him their backstage passes. Walking around the stage, they found the entrance to the narrow hall that led to the dressing rooms. Sam assumed each member of Bodies in Motion would have his own dressing room, but that wasn't the case. There was one door with the name of the band taped to it. Outside the door was another security guard in a blue uniform and hat, this one more stocky than the last. Once more they proudly flashed their passes.

The guard looked Sam and Erik up and down, then said, "Just a minute." The guard walked into the dressing room, closing the door behind him.

"Shit, he must have to make sure they're dressed," Erik said.

An image of all four members of the band standing around naked flashed through Sam's mind. He didn't think the guard was making sure the boys were dressed, but assumed they would be wearing something when they stepped inside. The door opened again and the guard appeared. He looked Sam and Erik over once more.

"Go on in," the guard said.

Sam was the first to walk inside and take a look around the large white walled room. A shelf ran along the wall on the right and had a mirror above it. Across the room was a rack full of clothes. The boys were still dressed in the clothes they'd worn for the show. Ed sat in one of the chairs closest to the door, and swivelled the chair around. He took a good look at Erik, then grinned.

"Isn't this a pleasant surprise," Justin said, stepping away from the clothes rack and walking towards them in his stockinged feet. Stopping in the middle of the room, he crossed his arms and his full lips spread into a smile. "Who won the passes?"

"I did," Sam said, holding back a stupid grin and a scream. Sam knew his boner was obvious, as was Erik's, but neither of them could help themselves. He stepped forward and extended his hand. When Justin shook it, he thought he was going to blow a load.

Erik lunged forward and shook Justin's hand as he

introduced himself.

"You guy's seem pleased to be here," Ted said, leaning against the wall to the left. He scratched his arm, then stepped forward. He motioned towards the door to his left. "Kurt will be out in a bit. He had to take a leak."

There was a flush, then the bathroom door opened. Kurt looked both Sam and Erik over, then grinned. "Ted thinks everyone needs to know my business," Kurt said, running his fingers through his short bangs. He stepped up to Sam and shook his hand, then did the same to Erik. "How did you boys like the show?"

A blush rose on Sam's cheeks at the mention of him being a boy. "It was real good," he managed to spit out, then began to grin uncontrollably. "I can't believe I'm back here with you guys. This is so great."

"Why don't you guys hang with us for a bit while we change up," Justin said, motioning to the overstuffed sofa against the wall to the left. He grabbed hold of the bottom of his t-shirt then lifted it over his head. Justin's stomach was firm, his pectorals well defined. Ted and Kurt also began to undress, both of them exposing tight swimmers builds.

Erik gave Sam a nudge, then leaned in close and whispered, "You're drooling."

Sam wiped his lower lip, only to find that Erik had been kidding. He was staring, but who could blame him. His favorite boy band was undressing in front of him. Ed was down to his blue and white plaid boxer shorts, his cock swaying back and forth beneath the cotton material. It looked semi-hard.

Sam followed Erik to the sofa, then took a seat to his left. Justin let his pants drop, then stepped out of them. Behind the white cotton briefs, Justin's shaft bulged out. His big balls helped to form a nice package. It was getting to be too much for Sam to watch, his cock was aching for release.

"Do you guys want anything to drink?" Justin asked as he

walked up to them. Once he was inches from Erik he stopped and looked down at Sam, their eyes meeting.

"I'm fine,"Erik said.

Justin reached out and ran his fingers through Erik's dark hair. "It's going to be great to hang out with you guys."

"This is so cool," Sam blurted out, then hoped he didn't look like too much of a nerd.

"What about you?" Justin said as he winked at Sam. "Is there anything you would like?"

"Don't be shy now," Ted said, coming up behind Justin and slipping his hands around Justin's waist, feeling his torso. Gradually, his hands roamed the wide expanse of tight muscle before his right hand dipped into the elastic waist band of Justin's briefs and around his shaft and balls. Ted kissed Justin's neck. Justin let out a sigh, then tilted his head back.

Sam was speechless as Ed walked up to him and slipped out of his boxer shorts. His thick nine inch shaft swayed semi-hard in front of his face, a purple vein running along the length. His big balls were in a tight sack beneath his swelling meat. Sam gripped his cock at the base then licked a bead of pre-cum off the ripe head. As Sam began to suck, he felt Ed's hand on the back of his head. Ed moved his hips forward, slowly easing his fleshy fuck stick down Sam's eager gullet. Sam gulped and swallowed until the entire length was down his throat, then felt Ed's shaft slowly ease out of his mouth.

"Oh fuck," Ed called out, only to be muffled when Kurt gave him a kiss.

With Ed's cock fucking his mouth, Sam reached up and touched Kurt's cock as it rubbed against Ed's thigh. Pre-cum oozed out of Kurt's piss slit, forming a wet trail on Ed's skin. Ed's cock head was beginning to swell, getting ready to burst, when Ed told Sam to stop. Ed pulled his prick out of Sam's mouth and held onto it.

"Why don't you get out of those clothes," Kurt said to Sam.

Sam's lips were wet from sucking Ed's meat as he stood, pulled off his shirt, then stepped out of his jeans. Erik was already naked, leaning forward with his hands on his knees while Justin slammed his thick, latex wrapped cock in and out of his ass. Ted held onto Erik's head as he fed him his shaft.

Sam felt someone's hands on his ass, spreading his cheeks. There was moisture on his hole, and a tongue tickling his pucker. Kurt went down on his knees and started sucking Sam's prick. The boys were trying so damn hard to get him off, but Sam wanted to hold back and enjoy the moment. He watched as Ted pulled his prick out of Erik's mouth and gave it a stroke. Every muscle in Ted's body tightened as a thick stream of cum spewed out of his piss slit and splattered on Erik's face, covering his cheek and dripping down his chin. He shot two more loads of creamy cum that coated Erik's face.

"Oh shit," Justin moaned as he slammed his cock deep inside Erik's ass and held still. Both Kurt and Ed stopped what they were doing to watch. Justin pulled his shaft back until it seemed as if only the head was inside, then slammed it back in. Slowly, Justin pulled his rod back, let out another groan, then crammed his stiff prick inside once more. After that Justin moved with short jabs up Erik's fuck chute and softly sighed and groaned as he spewing his load up Erik's ass.

Sam saw Erik's prick twitch, then Erik let out a groan. The first load of jizz shot out of Erik's swollen knob and splattered onto the floor as Justin pulled his dick out of Erik's butt hole. Erik let out another groan and continued to spew his frothy load.

Both Ed and Kurt continued to stroke their meat as Sam went down on his knees and sucked one cock, then the other. Both boys were into it, reaching over Sam's head to pinch each other's nipples and kiss.

"Let me see you suck his cock," Ed said.

Sam worked on Kurt's dick, sucking the entire length down, then extracting it from his throat in one continuous movement. And as he watched, Ed continued to stroke his rod, a clear stream of pre-cum drooling out of his piss slit.

"Oh man," Ed hissed, then stepped back. Sam felt a warm splash of Ed's spunk hit his chest, then another against his neck.

"Oh man," Kurt whispered as he pulled his dick out of Sam's mouth. Cum drooled out, over Sam's fingers as he gripped the shaft and began stroking it. Without warning, a shot spit out and hit Sam in the chin. Another glob of spunk splattered on his chest, mixing with Ed's creamy load. The rest of Kurt's load slowed drooled out until he was spent.

Sam leaned back and stroked his boner. It didn't take long for him to shoot his load on his stomach while the boys of Bodies in Motion watched, along with Erik. When he finished, the boys began to hoot and clap. For Sam it was a dream come true. He couldn't stop smiling.

"Next time we're around we'll let you know," Justin said. "We'll hook you up with free passes, and you can come back and visit."

"No way," Sam said, trying hard not to sound excited, but unable to hold back his emotions.

"Sure, man," Kurt said. "You guys are cool."

For Sam it couldn't get any better than that.

UPLOAD

Morning was never Jeremy's favorite time of day, especially now, waking up on the floor of one of hundreds of abandoned houses out in the suburbs. There was a chill in the air, but not enough to make Jeremy dread the day any more than he already did. His stiff prick pushed out against the fabric of his jeans, forming a long, thick bulge running down his left thigh. Jeremy scratched his muscular chest through the thick, synthetic shirt as he looked through the shards of broken glass clinging to the inside ridge of a window. The sun was shining down along a deserted street. Wind gently pushed trash along the dead lawns of homes that would never see life again. His craft, a green, rounded, tubular vehicle, was still parked in front of the house. Sure, sometimes squatters came to the suburbs for a while, hoping to make a home and perhaps outsmart the hounds that roamed the deserted suburbs. Unfortunately none of the squatters who tried to live in the suburbs were able to find a way of getting rid of the hounds. There were more hounds than humans, and the hound population was growing at an amazing rate.

Jeremy didn't bother exploring the house for fear of finding the final remains of one of the thousands of squatters whose dead bodies littered many of the empty houses. He hoped to get a move on before the hounds began their rounds, looking for fresh meat. He'd heard stories of how the hounds traveled in packs, often searching out a person traveling alone.

Jeremy slid his hands under his shirt, his rough palms exploring the left side of his rib cage, where the previous night's trick had inserted a small memory cartridge containing information he knew nothing about. Jeremy could almost feel the small device nestled snugly between two of his ribs. There was a small, metallic hole that seemed to be for something to plug into. Jeremy didn't really understand how the device worked, he just wanted the thing out of his body. "That fucker," Jeremy mumbled as he pulled his hand out from under his shirt. He tried to remember the guy's name that had the unit inserted, but couldn't.

When Jeremy had met the guy all he'd wanted to do was get off. He hadn't regretted the sex. Hell, the guy had been hot. Jeremy had been standing on one of the mesh platforms hovering above the dance floor at a club called The Zone when he'd noticed the guy standing along the outer edge of the dance floor. Vibrant colors had blazed over his tight body, showing off his lean frame through a tight T-shirt and shorts. It had been then that Jeremy decided to meet him.

The pick up was easy. It seemed like the guy was more than willing to trick with Jeremy as long as it was at his place, not Jeremy's apartment. Jeremy agreed and off they went.

As it turned out, the guy lived in a house in a wealthy neighborhood. The rooms were large, spacious, and minimally furnished. Looking up, Jeremy noticed that each floor was on a tier so that if you were on the third floor you could look over the balcony and view the two floors below.

Jeremy followed his trick to the bedroom on the third

floor. Once there, both men slowly undressed. Jeremy liked the way the guy's cock and balls spilled out of his shorts, hanging low and ready.

"What's your name?" the guy asked.

"Jeremy."

"Your friends call you Jerry?"

"No, they call me Jere," Jeremy said. He didn't care what this guy's name was. All he wanted to do was get off.

Walking up to the man, Jeremy pressed his chest against the guy's body. As the two men kissed, Jeremy slid his open palms down the guy's back and over the curve of his tight ass. Then, slipping his fingers between the firm mounds of ass, he eased his middle finger towards his tight, hot fuck hole. Pressing the tip of his middle finger against the wrinkled opening, Jeremy felt it give way and allow his finger to penetrate.

Their lips parted. The man slid down Jeremy's body and licked the head of his prick, then ran his index finger along the serpentine vein that ran along the side of Jeremy's dick. Jeremy liked the feeling of the guy's tongue on his cock head and was eager to watch this guy suck his cock. Grabbing hold of the guy's hair and pulling his face away from his prick, Jeremy asked, "You think you can take it?"

"Sure."

Jeremy snickered to himself, knowing how many guys had eagerly taken his cock down their throats only to find that they couldn't give a steady blow job. He hoped this guy wouldn't be another one of them "Then go ahead, suck my cock."

Jeremy felt his shaft slowly slide down the guy's throat. The guy gently tugged on Jeremy's balls as he pumped his face up and down on his cock. Closing his eyes and biting his lower lip, Jeremy couldn't believe how well the guy sucked dick. He felt cum rise up his shaft, building at the head, getting ready to explode. Grabbing the guy's head, he pulled his cock out of his throat.

"Slow down, man," Jeremy said. "Shit, I still want to fuck your hot ass."

The guy stood away from Jeremy, exposing his stiff prick rising up towards his navel. "Why don't we try the bed then," the man said.

Jeremy looked over at the bed. "Sure, why not," he said. They both walked over to the bed, where they sprawled out. Jeremy placed his hand over the guy's back then slid it over his ass.

"There are some condoms on the night stand, if you want to use one," the man said.

Reaching out, Jeremy took the plastic wrapped latex condom from the night stand and put it between his teeth. Although a cure for AIDS had been found, there were more than a few people who didn't trust the government enough to stop using condoms. Jeremy was one of them.

Jeremy unrolled a latex sheath over his shaft as the guy rolled onto his stomach and spread his legs. Reaching towards the guy, Jeremy spread his firm ass cheeks, exposing his tight fuck hole. He slapped his dick against the wrinkled hole, watching it tighten then relax. Jeremy began to lube up the guy's pucker, poking two fingers inside and feeling the tight ring of muscle grip his digits. He couldn't wait to stick his prick inside and start pumping away, feeling the warmth of his fuck chute and the tight ass ring grip his shaft. The guy moaned and raised his ass in the air as Jeremy fingered his hole.

"Take it slow on my ass, it's been a while since I took a cock up there, " the man said.

"Don't worry," Jeremy said as he pressed the head of his cock against the guy's tight pucker. The hole opened to Jeremy's bulbous cock head, then wrapped around it and gulped it down.

"Oh yeah," the guy said.

Get ready to open that fucking hole, Jeremy thought as he began to press inch after inch of his ten thick inches of meat deep inside the guy's bowels. Once inside, Jeremy held his cock still for a few minutes, feeling the man's body heat on his shaft and the way his sphincter gripped his prick.

Slowly, Jeremy began easing his cock out of the guy's fuck hole, pulling back until only the head was inside, then gliding his length back inside. The guy moaned approvingly as he eased himself up on all fours and begged to be fucked harder. Jeremy took hold of the guy's hips and began fucking him faster, feeling his hips slam into his firm ass cheeks with each inward plunge.

Jeremy liked the way this guy fucked, moving away as he pulled out and pushing towards him as he slammed his shaft all the way up his silky smooth bowels. Hot cum filled Jeremy's shaft, building up at the head, getting ready to burst. Biting his lower lip, Jeremy tried to hold back as he continued to thrust. Soon he knew it would happen. He was about to cum. Letting out a deep groan, Jeremy felt his cock head pulse and spew his thick load up the guy's ass. With each thrust he felt spunk shoot out of his piss slit until it slowed, then stopped.

Letting out a final sigh, Jeremy pulled his cock out of the guy's ass, then fell back on the bed. The guy straddled Jeremy's chest so his big balls rested against his neck. Slowly, the guy began stroking his shaft. Jeremy watched as the head of his cock became ripe and swollen in front of him and knew that it would not be long before he blew his load.

"Oh fuck," the guy said as he shot his spunk all over Jeremy's face.

"Well, what have we here," a low, male voice said from behind the man straddling Jeremy's chest.

Jeremy had felt a cold hand against his rib cage, then a prick. Everything had gone black.

Jeremy shivered from the memory. If only he could rip the

implant out of his ribs, but he knew that doing so was impossible. Those fuckers were secret agents and they had knocked him out, filled an implant chip with information and set it between his ribs.

When he'd woken up the three secret agents had been watching him. It had only been then that Jeremy had been able to get a good look at the two guys he hadn't seen before, only heard. One was short and plump with big ears and the other tall and muscular with thick lips, a receding hair line and a scar that ran from the corner of his left eye to his mouth. They told him that he had two choices, either deliver the information to a designated man by the name of Sid or be arrested for murder. They even showed him some of the evidence that would be used against him.

It seemed as if Jeremy had no choice, so he agreed. He was told that Sid could be found in Boston. They handed Jeremy an address written on a book of matches.

"It's a bar," the plump guy said. "Just go up to the bar tender and ask for Sid. He'll point you in the right direction."

The guy with the scar smiled grimly. "And don't try to run away. We know all about you, from birth until now," he said. "We know that you have no home and no real friends. Well, except for Hal Lockland, who you only see about once a year. You're not involved in anything illegal, unless you were hustling five years ago, before such things became legalized, which it doesn't seem that you were. Then there's your agent, David Blum, who you only speak with on the phone to get work. Face it, you're just a hustler who occasionally fucks a guy for his own pleasure, no money changing hands. You see, Jeremy, to us you're just an easy target."

"And then?" Jeremy asked as he pocketed the matches.

"Then what?" scar man asked.

"Will you guys take this implant out of me?"

Scar man had sneered as he looked at Jeremy. "Yeah, yeah, sure."

So now Jeremy had to make his way to Boston and deliver the information that had been planted in his body to a man he knew nothing about. It was a bum wrap and he had no choice but to deal with it. Those fuckers, he thought as he walked to the front door and opened it.

"Sid," Jeremy whispered as he stepped outside, keeping an eye out for hounds as he walked to his craft. He unlocked the driver's side door and slipped behind the wheel. The door closed with a dull thud as he saw a pack of hounds slowly inching their way around the corner of an abandoned house. Jeremy put the key in the ignition, pumped the accelerator and set the craft to lift off. The craft gently eased off the ground as the hounds began barking and running towards the craft. Jeremy flipped the drive switch, pressed his foot on the accelerator and sped off.

The on ramp to the highway was a few miles away, and the scenery didn't change all that much. Jeremy kept his eyes on the road, which was better than looking at rotting lawns and abandoned split level houses. Jeremy felt his prick stiffening in his jeans. What he needed now was a good fuck, but wasn't sure whom he could trust. Masturbation seemed his only relief, but that was something he never cared for doing. He grabbed his crotch, feeling the solid tube of flesh through cotton.

The communicator rang and Jeremy pressed the answer button and said hello. "Jere, where are you now?" It was Hal.

"Connecticut." Jeremy said.

"Connecticut? I thought you were going to be in New York for a while. What, some john going to shell out decent cash to cut your vacation short?" Hal said, sounding a bit annoyed.

"Something like that," Jeremy said, forcing a laugh. He didn't want to get Hal mixed up in all this espionage shit. Anyone can tap a phone line.

"Isn't that just like you, cash before friends, you greedy fucker," Hal said, a slight chuckle in his voice. "You better be coming back. You can't just blow off a friend like this."

"Don't worry, I'll be back. Give me a day or so," Jeremy said. "I can't let this one go." The on ramp to the highway was up ahead. Jeremy steered onto the ramp and slipped into traffic. "I'll let you know when I'll be back."

"And you better stay around a bit longer so we can get together."

"Sure will, Hal."

"Be good."

Jeremy pressed the hang-up button then turned on the radio and tried to forget about everything, but it was no use. All he could think about was Hal and how he wished he could be with Hal now, feeling his soft flesh against him, sucking Hal's big, hairy balls into his mouth. Jeremy was known for being a top, but when it came to Hal, Jeremy would bottom. For Hal he would raise his legs in the air so Hal could fuck him up the ass good and hard. It wasn't because Hal's prick was small or thin, because it wasn't. Hal's cock was easily nine inches, although not quite as thick as Jeremy's.

The first time Hal had fucked Jeremy it had hurt some, despite the fact that Hal had eased his prick inside Jeremy nice and slow. But once Jeremy's fuck chute was able to conform to the size of Hal's dick, everything went well.

Usually, after Hal fucked Jeremy, the two of them would relax and have a chat. Post fuck had always been a pleasant, relaxing time for them. They'd talk about whatever was on their minds. Jeremy wished he could talk to Hal now. Hal would know what to do about this espionage stunt that he's being forced to pull off.

To Jeremy, Boston was just another dark city with flashing neon and too many people. From a distance you could tell one city from the others, but once you were deep inside you could be in any one of the capital cities scattered across the country and never know the difference. There had once been a time when every city had its own personality, but that had gone long ago. Now every city in every state had the same stores, the same cinemas and the same street layout. Anyone could go into any city and know how to get around. Despite the fact that all subway stops and streets had different names, it was a simplicity that took away individuality.

Jeremy shifted onto the exit ramp and into Boston. The first thing Jeremy wanted to do when he finished with this little endeavor was get back to New York and forget all about the implant and Sid and get back to his life. Maybe when he arrived in New York he could give his agent a call and see if perhaps he couldn't make a few bucks while he was there. Hell, he would still be able to spend time with Hal! Or so he hoped.

Jeremy parked in the twenty-five story lot across from the Swan Plaza Hotel. The club wasn't far. He figured he could easily take the subway to the bar where he was going to meet Sid. Jeremy went to the subway stop on the corner and walked down the stairs leading underground. A glass booth sat in the center of a platform. Behind that were two sets of stairs, one for Science Park and the other for Boston College, Cleveland Circle, Riverside. He paid the fair and asked when the next train would arrive. The greasy man in the booth told him in about fifteen minutes as he slid the token at him. Time enough to take a piss, Jeremy thought.

The men's room was gray and smelled of piss and cum. A man in a dark suit had followed Jeremy inside and sidled up to the urinal next to him. Jeremy pulled out his pecker, looked at the beige tile in front of him, then began to take a leak.

Sneaking a peek at the urinal beside him, Jeremy took a look at the guy's dick. The guy didn't seem to mind. In fact, he took a step back as if to show off his small cock with a tapered head as it spit out a steady stream of urine. Jeremy caught the man's eye, then motioned with his head towards the toilet stalls.

Shaking the final drops of piss from his prick, the man moved away from the urinal and into the first in a line of five stalls. Jeremy followed him inside, then closed the door behind him. The lock on the door was broken, but Jeremy didn't care. All he wanted was to get his dick sucked.

Jeremy felt the man grope his crotch, then reach inside his fly and pull out his massive cock. Jeremy stood still, feeling the guy's fingers wrapped around his prick. Knowing he didn't have time for foreplay, Jeremy looked the guy square in the face and said, "Suck it."

The man went to his knees and sucked Jeremy's stiffening cock down his throat. Jeremy felt his prick engulfed in the guy's throat, his tongue rubbing against the underbelly of his shaft. Jeremy took in a deep breath as the man brought Jeremy to the point of ejaculation, then stopped. He pulled Jeremy's dick out of his mouth and looked up at him, his thin lips wet with spit.

"Come on, man," Jeremy said.

The door to the men's room opened, then there were footfalls heading towards the toilet stalls. Jeremy leaned against the door, grabbed his shaft and began to stroke himself to orgasm. Splattering his frothy cum over the man's face, Jeremy watched as the guy tried to grab hold of his legs. Jeremy let out a grunt as the final drops of his spunk spilled out of his cock. The guy in front of him tried to hold onto Jeremy's legs once more. Jeremy kicked him in the stomach, then lost his footing. Pressing his palms against the toilet stall walls, Jeremy steadied himself.

The toilet stall door flew open. Jeremy turned in time to see a lumbering hulk of a man lunge at him. Jeremy kicked the man in the balls as the man who had blown him reached up and grabbed his waist. Stepping back, Jeremy shoved the cock sucker away from him, sending his head crashing against the toilet bowl. The man behind Jeremy regained balance. Jeremy turned and lunged towards him, grabbing him by the throat and shoving him against the tiled wall. The man's head hit the wall with a crack, knocking him unconscious.

Jeremy ran out of the men's room as the train slid along its monorail track and screeched to a halt. The doors slid open and people spilled onto the platform. Jeremy pushed into a crowd of people waiting to enter the train as the door to the men's room opened and one of the goons shot out and looked around. Moving with the crowd as they boarded the train, Jeremy tried to stay low and out of sight. Once on the train, Jeremy saw the goon from the men's room scanning the windows of the train. Jeremy crouched down, out of view. All around him people boarded the train, not paying any attention to him. They must think I'm a fucking freak, Jeremy thought. Watching both entrances, he hoped the man wouldn't board the train. As it was all the seats were taken and people were standing around him, blocking his view of the entrances. Then the doors closed with a shutter. Jeremy stood and looked out the window, catching a brief glimpse of a solitary man standing on the platform as the train jolted forward, then sped away.

Only two men sat at the bar, both looking lonely and contemplative. By their worn and out of style clothes, Jeremy figured they were both unemployed. What other type of guy would haunt a bar during off hours? It was a depressing place, and the maroon walls didn't help any. Jeremy sauntered up to the bar, took a seat and waited. The bartender, a short, muscular man in a tight t-shirt was stocking the back shelf with various bottles of liquor. He looked over at Jeremy, then slowly walked up to him.

"What can I do for you?" the bartender asked, his voice raw and street wise.

"I'm looking for Sid," Jeremy said.

The bartender looked Jeremy over. "He expecting you?"

"Yes," Jeremy answered.

The bartender looked across the dimly lit room, past the small square of the dance floor, at a door smack in the center of the far wall. "See that door. Go inside and up the stairs. You'll see him."

Jeremy nodded then made his way to the door, which opened on a set of smoked glass stairs lit from underneath. At the top of the stairs was nothing but a black wall.

"Come in," said a familiar voice that Jeremy couldn't quite place. "Just step through that wall, it's just an illusion."

Jeremy stepped through the darkness, walking into a large, well lit room. Across from him was a cherry wood desk facing him. Seated in a high back leather chair was the man with the scar who had handed him the address to this bar. Jeremy couldn't believe what he was seeing. Could all of this been a farce?

"Yes, I am Sid," the man behind the desk said, pressing his fingertips together.

"What's this all about?" Jeremy asked.

"A little confused are we? Well, let me explain it all to you. You see, you did very well. I wasn't sure you were as tough as I'd been told. You proved me wrong. I'm impressed and so is the board."

"The board?

"Yes," Sid continued. "The people who help keep this program in operation. There are only four of us. You've met three. You see, the board has plans for you. These plans include offering you a job. A government job. Top secret."

"And if I don't want to take your job?"

"That's up to you. But first, let me explain what we would like to do. As you know we specialize in the transferring of information from one place to another using humans. This is very confidential material that we transport and we do not want it found out or traced, which, if we used the normal methods of electronic transmission, would be an easy task for anyone wishing to intercept us. Are you following me?"

Jeremy nodded.

"We want to place a memory chip deep inside your intestines, about nine inches from your asshole. Once set, we upload the chip with information."

"You already stuck one of those damn things inside me, why another?"

"Oh, no, no we did not install a memory unit inside you yet. Did we say that we did? Forgive us, we were mistaken. What we installed inside you is a unit that monitors your heart rate and blood pressure. It can also make your heart stop beating if we decide to do that, that is." Sid leaned back in his chair and smiled.

Jeremy held back his anger, knowing that a fight wouldn't get him anywhere fast. "So, guess I have little choice then."

"No, you have two choices," Sid said.

"Sure, live or die, right?"

"If that's how you want to label them," Sid said, looking directly at Jeremy. "So tell me, have you made up your mind?"

The operation didn't take long. Jeremy was placed on his back, his arms held out and strapped up with leather restraints. Wires connected his chest to monitors that beeped and blipped on small screens. His legs were bound to metal rods that held them apart, his asshole exposed to the surgeon in the green gown with matching surgical mask and head covering.

"It's best if you don't look," the surgeon said.

Jeremy felt cold metal pressed against his asshole. He took a deep breath, closed his eyes and tried to relax. More cold metal was being inserted into his pucker, then he felt his hole being stretched. Jeremy let out a groan as he tried to relax.

"Take a deep breath and hold it," the surgeon said.

Another cold, metallic object was inserted up his ass. Then Jeremy felt his sphincter being stretched open even more. Jeremy took in another deep breath and held it, then let out the breath slowly when the stretching stopped.

"That's not too bad," the surgeon said as he walked out from between Jeremy's legs. He held up a syringe with a three inch needle attached to the tip.

"What are you doing?" Jeremy asked.

"You do not want to be awake when we insert the memory chip into your intestines. It won't be very pleasant for you, so we're putting you under," the surgeon said as he walked across the room. He came back with a moist cotton swab and rubbed it on the crook of Jeremy's arm.

Jeremy closed his eyes as he felt the needle being inserted into his arm. He was knocked out cold by the time the needle was removed.

After a week of rest Jeremy was fully recovered from the operation. Sid explained where he would be living and gave him a set of keys to his new craft. The old one had exploded when a bomb went off in the parking lot where he'd left his car. A body had been found, identified as his and buried, closed casket, in the a small cemetery just outside of Providence, RI. He was now untraceable.

Naked, Jeremy was sent to Sid's office for his first assignment. He padded down the white hallway to the office, only to find Sid leaning against his desk with an erection. Jeremy couldn't help but look at Sid's cock, which was eleven inches long and at least seven in circumference.

"The head of my cock contains the information that will be uploaded into you. You should find this pleasurable," Sid said, scratching the hair on his well defined chest.

Jeremy's eyes finally drifted up, past Sid's erection. He looked around the room, at the lack of furniture or wall hangings.

"If you could please put your hands against the wall I will get you ready for the upload," Sid said.

Jeremy did as he was told, feeling the cold wall against his palms as he spread his legs. Feeling Sid lube his pucker, he hoped he would enter him slowly. Sid walked up behind him and rubbed the head of his cock across Jeremy's ass crack.

"Go slow," Jeremy said.

"Feeling a little tight, Jere?" Sid said, then pressed his cock head against Jeremy's pucker.

Jeremy took in a breath as he felt Sid's knobby cock head pushing against his asshole, then felt his sphincter stretch open wide to accommodate the girth of Sid's shaft. Slowly, the rest of Sid's prick inched inside Jeremy's bowels. Jeremy groaned as a sharp pain gripped his guts. Sid continued to insert his cock up Jeremy's asshole despite his obvious discomfort. Jeremy closed his eyes and tried to clear his mind, but all he could feel was the massive girth of Sid's meat opening his bowels.

Once the entire length of Sid's prick was lodged up Jeremy's ass, Sid paused, placed his hands firmly on Jeremy's hips and slowly began to slide his shaft in and out of his tight pucker. The pain had subsided, leaving Jeremy to experience the sliding motion of Sid's shaft against his sphincter. There was also a small, almost undetectable pulsing deep inside his bowels as information was uploaded into the implant. Jeremy's dick gradually rose to attention as Sid continued to fuck him in a steady rhythm.

Pre-cum drooled out of the head of Jeremy's prick, dripping onto the floor and causing a small pool of clear fuck fluid to form between his legs. Jeremy couldn't believe how turned on he was from getting fucked. Relaxing his asshole, Jeremy felt his fuck stick twitch with excitement as his cock head became ripe and swollen. Without touching his prick, he felt as if he was about to cum. As his shaft began to jerk, Jeremy let out a groan. Jeremy's thick, ripe cock head pulsed, spitting out globs of cum that hit the wall and slowly dripped down to the floor.

Sid let out a guttural groan, pulled his shaft out of Jeremy's ass, gave his prick a few strokes and came on Jeremy's ass.

"You have the information, now go to your chamber and clean up," Sid said once he'd finished ejaculating. "We will meet you in the briefing room in an hour."

"What kind of information am I carrying?" Jeremy asked, feeling his asshole begin to close.

"That is something you don't need to know. Your job is to transport this information from one place to another without being traced." Sid walked towards his desk, keeping an eye on Jeremy.

"But, don't I get a chance to find out what I'm carrying?"

"Don't worry, you will be rewarded handsomely. Trips, men, cars. All you have to do is work for us and everything will be taken care of."

"But I can't go back," Jeremy said.

"Well, that's just a minor inconvenience. After all, you are dead."

Jeremy looked at Sid, then realized he had no choice. He had to do what they wanted or they would have him killed.

HANGING OUT

Alan watched as Victor lay back on the grass, moonlight glowing on his tanned upper torso. Victor's chest was smooth and narrow, like a swimmer's. Slowly tearing apart a leaf, Victor looked up at the night sky, then let the small pieces drift onto his chest. He turned towards Alan and smiled, exposing a mouth of slightly crooked teeth. Without saying a word, Victor reached out and rubbed the top of Alan's bare foot, moving up towards the dark hairs that covered his leg. Although both boys had deep brown skin, Alan's color wasn't from laying out in the sun. Through Victor's thin cotton shorts, Alan saw the outline of his long, slender prick as it began to stiffen.

Alan and Victor had started jerking each other off after Victor's eighteenth birthday. Alan, who had already turned eighteen, had spent the night at Victor's house, where the two of them shared a bed. Feeling horny and curious, Alan had slipped his hand on Victor's thigh and asked Victor if he knew what older guys did with each other. Victor had looked nervous and curious, but still he said that he didn't need to know.

"Come on, let me show you," Alan had said. "Pull down your undies."

Victor had hesitantly pulled his briefs down, then held his breath. Alan had wrapped his fingers around Victor's prick, feeling it in his grip. It had been so exciting for him, as if they'd been doing something very bad. There had also been the impending doom of Victor's parents in the other room. As Alan had stroked Victor's cock, all he'd been able to think about was what would happen if Victor's parents walked in. Luckily they hadn't then, nor had they been caught any of the other times they'd played with each other.

There was the sound of tires crunching gravel. Alan knew it was Victor's next door neighbor, Mr. DeLuca, coming home. Alan hoped he had his handsome blond friend with him. Both Alan and Victor knew that the two men fucked around with each other. Alan had even caught glimpses of them doing it once through Mr. DeLuca's bedroom window.

"You have to do it with me," Alan whispered.

Victor's brown eyes widened. "What if we get caught?" he asked. "The Robinson's house is right next door."

Alan rolled his eyes, then looked over at the blue raised ranch that was just past Mr. DeLuca's green ranch. None of the lights in the Robinson's house were on, which meant they weren't home. Not only that, but there were some bushes outside Mr. DeLuca's bedroom window that were tall enough to hide them.

"The bushes will hide us from the Robinson's house and we'll be far enough from the street not to be noticed. Plus it's dark. Come on," Alan said.

"Let's wait," Victor said.

Alan looked out at the green ranch. The kitchen window lit up.

"Alan," Victor whined.

"Come on, let's go," Alan said, then stood and slowly

made his way into Mr. DeLuca's yard. Lucky for Alan, Victor's parents had never put up a fence.

Victor followed close behind Alan as they walked up to the rear of Mr. DeLuca's house, then crouched down and went around to the side. The bushes were directly behind them, the tiny stiff branches tickling their backs.

They were in luck, the bedroom window was open and the screen was down. Alan glanced inside the dark room, making out the shapes of the bed to the right and a bureau against the far wall. The light turned on, and Alan felt Victor's hand grip his shoulder. Both boys ducked lower. Mr. DeLuca stepped into the room, naked. What luck, Alan thought. A thick tuft of dark hair covered Mr. DeLuca's well defined pectorals, and a thin line of it trailed down the middle of his chest and spilled into his pubic hair. Mr. DeLuca's long, thick shaft lobbed in front of his big, low hanging balls. Laying down on the bed, Mr. DeLuca gently ran his fingertips over the length of his hardening shaft, which to Alan looked to be a good eight inches.

"Hey there," Mr. DeLuca's blond friend said as he leaned against the door frame with his arms folded. The blond's stiff dick matched Mr. DeLuca's in width, but was an inch shorter in length. His balls were also held in a tight sack, unlike Mr. DeLuca's.

Mr. DeLuca slid down on the bed as his friend walked up to him, then got on the bed and grabbed the headboard as he knelt over Mr. DeLuca's face. Pressing his big hands against the blond's ass, Mr. DeLuca separated his cheeks, then started licking his asshole.

Alan's prick shifted in his shorts as he watched Victor's neighbor rim his friend. He wondered how it felt to lick an asshole, and wished he'd had the balls to tell Victor that he'd love to lick his asshole.

Alan unzipped his shorts, then pulled out his stiff prick. Grabbing his shaft in the middle, he stroked up so the foreskin covered the head. A thin strand of pre-cum drooled out of the piss slit and hit the ground. Victor also had his dick out, and was slowly stroking it as he watched Mr. Deluca eat out his buddy's hole. Alan reached out and batted Victor's hand away from his shaft, then spit in his hand and started to stroke Victor's cut cock. Looking back in, Alan watched as Mr. DeLuca sucked the blond's tight nuts into his mouth. The blond guy was stroking his shaft, his head tilted back.

Victor's head jerked back, and a soft gasp escaped his lips. Alan felt Victor's shaft pulse in his grip, then saw the first shot a thick spunk hit the side of Mr. DeLuca's house. Alan continued to stroke Victor's prick as more and more jizz spewed out, hitting the side of the house before the bursts slowed.

Now it was Alan's turn to shoot. Victor's fist continued to stroke Alan's rod as he watched Mr. DeLuca suck his friend's stiff dick. He imagined the blond was Victor and he was Mr. DeLuca. Then he felt the hot spunk filling his prick, turning the head into a swollen knob ready to burst. His legs tightened, then he let the first shot fly.

That night all Alan could think about was how he'd seen Mr. DeLuca doing stuff he'd always wanted to do with Victor but had been too afraid to admit. Under the sheets Alan's dick was rock hard, rising up big and thick, the foreskin half covering the ripe head. Alan ran his fingers through his dark pubic hair, feeling his hard cock against the back of his hand. With his other hand he played with his asshole, rubbing his middle and index fingers against the tight puckered opening and feeling the warm moisture. Alan wanted to smell Victor's fuck hole, then tickle it with the tip of his tongue. He wanted to lay his tongue flat against the hole and feel it pucker up.

Taking his fingers away from his ass, Alan brought them up to his nose and inhaled the intoxicating scent of his hole.

They smelled deep and musty. He licked the fingers that he'd pressed against his ass, hoping to get a taste of his fuck hole.

Grabbing hold of his stiff rod, Alan began to slowly stroke. The next time he was alone with Victor he would get his lips on his ass. No more just jerking each other off, Alan thought. He wanted to eat Victor's ass, lick his hole and suck his balls. Alan also wanted to feel his shaft ease up Victor's fuck chute. He wanted to feel the warmth and tightness of Victor's ass.

Alan's body tightened, and he readied his free hand around his swollen cock head. He stroked down, then up. His legs tightened, then the first blast of hot cum spewed out of his piss slit and into his hand. Quickly, he brought his hand to his mouth, smearing the thick jizz over his lips, and onto his tongue. Another blast of fuck juice spewed onto his stomach as he licked his cum covered fingers.

Alan's parents were out for the night, and so was his older brother, Ross. It was the perfect time to invite Victor over, so Alan had called and told him to drop by so they could hang out. Alan felt a little guilty for having invited Victor over under false pretenses. What Alan really wanted to do with Victor was eat his ass, suck his cock and maybe even fuck him up the ass. Alan's shorts were tight just thinking about actually doing some real stuff with Victor. He paced the living room, feeling the plush carpet beneath his bare feet as he walked past the dark wood coffee table once more. He had to stop his pacing, so he sat down on the recliner, pushed back so his feet were elevated on the foot rest and rubbed his bulging crotch. He glared at the large screen television. He didn't want to turn it on, although he'd told Victor that maybe they could just watch some television. Was anything worth watching even on? Alan didn't know. He hoped his hardon would go down before Victor arrived. The last thing he needed to do was open the door packing a chubby.

A cool breeze blew through the window to Alan's right, rustling the thin green curtains and allowing moonlight to shimmer in through the window. A family portrait hung above the deep blue sofa. The picture had been taken back when Alan was ten, and he looked so damn young and stupid in it. His brother had been eleven then, and his braces made him look like an even bigger goof than Alan.

Alan heard Victor's car pull up against the curb, then the engine shut off. The car door slammed shut. He would be at the door soon, Alan thought. He got up quickly and walked to the door. Trying to keep his boner as hidden as possible in his shorts, he pushed his hand inside and tried to reposition his shaft. There was nothing he could do. The doorbell rang, startling Alan. He dashed his hand out of his shorts, then threw open the door.

"Hey there," Victor said as he brushed past Alan, the back of his hand rubbing against Alan's stiff dick. "Is there anything good on tonight?"

"Haven't looked yet," Alan said, peeking at the bulge of meat between Victor's legs. He closed the door, then walked up to Victor. "We can do a little channel surfing, or just go and rent a movie."

"Or we could just hang," Victor said. He walked up to Alan and playfully tapped his stomach with his fist.

"Looking to start something, boy?" Alan said, holding Victor's stare and slapping his upper arm with the back of his hand. "Think you're so tough?"

"Oh yeah, I'm scared of you," Victor said, rolling his eyes. He stepped into the living room and kicked off his sandals. "Nobody's home?"

"Nobody," Alan said.

"I'm fucking horny." Victor grabbed his crotch, pushing his semi-stiff meat against the inside of his shorts. "It's this weather that does it to me. It's like driving me fucking bat shit."

Staring at Victor's bulging crotch, Alan could hardly contain himself. "How about going into my room," he said.

"Sure thing," Victor said. "Maybe a good jerk off session will do the trick."

The two boys raced upstairs and into Alan's bedroom. Once inside, Alan closed the door, then pulled off his shirt. Victor already had his shirt and shorts off, and Alan's eyes ran across his smooth skin. Alan slid out of his shorts, then his white boxers. Alan had to act cool, like he wasn't planning on doing anything out of the ordinary. He stepped up to the bed, pulled off his shirt and let it land on the floor. He unfastened his shorts and let them slide down his legs, where they bunched at his feet before he stepped out of them.

Alan stood in front of Victor wearing only his dark blue boxer shorts. Victor watched as Alan's cock and balls spilled out of his boxers, which he discarded with his shorts. Victor slid over, allowing space for Alan to spread out next to him.

Victor's body was warm and comforting, and Alan wanted to touch him so badly. Reaching out, Alan ran his fingers along the length of Victor's prick, down to his loose ball sack. To his surprise, Victor spread his legs. Alan dipped his fingers further down, running his index finger along the thin cord of flesh that ran down to Victor's asshole. Victor lifted his ass, then spread his legs wider.

"That feels good," Victor whispered as Alan pressed his middle and index fingers against the tight hole and rubbed. Victor's hand was on the back of Alan's neck, easing his face down to his crotch. "Lick my balls," Victor said.

Alan positioned himself between Victor's legs, grabbed his nuts, tightening the loose sack in his fist so the big globes were pushed out where his fingers met. Sticking out his tongue, he licked Victor's balls, then stuffed them in his mouth and let go of the fleshy pouch. Alan pulled back, then let Victor's balls pop out of his mouth. He dove down, then sucked each one back into his mouth, then pulled back until both balls popped out from between his lips once more.

Victor sighed and moaned, running his left foot along Alan's shoulder. The musky scent of Victor's ass rose up to greet Alan, teasing him with the desire to rim his friend. Alan pressed his thumbs against the tight hole, then gently pushed until the hole allowed the tip of his right thumb to penetrate. Victor lifted his ass slightly, which brought his fuck hole closer to Alan's lips. Alan's dick twitched with excitement. Slowly, Alan ran his tongue along the thin fleshy cord under his friend's nut sack.

"That feels good," Victor whispered.

It tasted good, too, Alan thought as he slipped his hands under the bottom of Victor's upper thighs and lifted his legs in the air. Victor's hole winked at him before Alan dove down and slapped his tongue against the puckered opening. Victor let out a groan as Alan licked the hole, feeling it contract against his tongue. Coming up for air briefly, Alan plunged back down and ran his tongue along the crack of Victor's ass. He gave the hole a kiss, then tickled it with the tip of his tongue

Pre-cum oozed out of Alan's piss slit and pooled on the top sheet. Alan knew if he grabbed his prick it would only take a few strokes before he shot his load. He didn't want that to happen, not yet at least. Alan wanted to shove his prick up Victor's ass and feel his bowls grip his rod.

Virgins no more, Alan thought. Not after this.

Sitting up, Alan wiped spit off his mouth before grabbing his cock, pulling back the fleshy hood and rubbing the head against the fleshy cord between Victor's legs. "You like that?" Alan asked.

"Yes," Victor said. "Rub your cock against my ass."

Reaching beneath the sheets, Alan grabbed the condom he'd hidden there and slipped it on. With slow, circular motions, Alan rubbed his cock head against Victor's hole. He pushed his knob against the hole, feeling it give way. Victor sighed, then lifted his legs higher. Alan pushed harder, feeling the hole open before he paused. Looking down, he saw his cock head about to plunge up his friend's ass. It was a beautiful sight.

"Put it in," Victor said, his voice soft and pleading.

Alan moved his hips back, watching as his prick lobbed up and down before pushing forward again so his swollen knob was against Victor's hole. He pressed gently once more, feeling the hole swallow his ripe head. With small thrusts, Alan eased his cock head in and out of Victor's hole.

"Put it in," Victor pleaded. "Come on, man. Give it to me."

Slowly, Alan pushed again, feeling Victor's ass ring stretch to fit his shaft. Victor's ass was warm and smooth around his pole. Victor's eyes tightened as Alan's prick eased up his ass. Alan felt Victor's ass ring grip his prick as more of it eased up Victor's fuck chute. He paused when he noticed Victor clenching his teeth.

"Give it to me," Victor said.

With one quick motion, Alan plunged his shaft inside until his balls slapped against Victor's ass. Alan held his position for a moment before beginning a slow, steady fuck. He watched Victor's face for signs of pain, but found none. Victor's lips were parted slightly, his eyes open and looking straight into Alan's as he grabbed his semi hard shaft and worked it back to full stiffness.

"You feel so good," Alan said.

Victor smiled, then dropped his legs onto Alan's shoulders, "Fuck me," he said.

Alan slowly pulled his shaft back until it was half way out, then gently slipped it back inside. Then he pulled back again until only the head was in before plunging back in.

"That feels so good," Victor said as he stroked his prick with the same slow motions of Alan's fuck stick.

Smooth, tight warmth surrounded Alan's rod as he moved it in and out in slow repetitions. He thought Victor's ass was amazing. Cum filled his shaft, building up at the head, causing Alan to close his eyes and try to hold back. Alan's breathing became heavy as his cock head swelled. Knowing he couldn't hold back any longer, Alan gritted his teeth then gave his shaft one final thrust before it shot its first hot load up Victor's ass. Alan let out a grunt, then pulled back. A second creamy load spewed from his piss slit, then a third. Alan shot another wad, then his body twitched, and he let out a sigh. The final bursts drooled out of Alan's cock as he slowed his movements down, then finally stopped.

Slowly, Alan pulled his prick out of Victor's ass, then licked the length of his friend's shaft before slipping the ripe head in his mouth. Alan shoved a few fingers into Victor's stretched hole, moving them in and out. The swollen head of Victor's prick scraped against Alan's gullet, almost causing him to gag. Pulling back, Alan sucked on the head, feeling it swell.

Taking Victor's cock out of his mouth, Alan gave it a stroke, then watched as the head pulsed and a thick glob of spunk shot out. Letting out a soft groan, Victor spewed his thick jizz onto his chest. Awestruck, Alan watched as load after creamy load shot out and covered Victor's chest and upper pecs.

Alan pulled Victor's prick out of his mouth, then withdrew his fingers from Victor's ass. "That was amazing," Alan said, bringing his fingers up to Victor's mouth. Victor licked Alan's fingers, then sucked them down his throat. Alan pulled back against the suction of Victor's mouth until his fingers slid out.

"Maybe next time the roles will be reversed," Victor said. "I'd love to feel my cock up your ass."

The sound of the front door closing echoed from downstairs. Shit, Alan thought. Luckily Alan's bedroom door was closed.

"Oh fuck," Victor whispered as heavy footsteps made their

way up to the second floor landing. The hallway floor creaked, then there was a knock at the door.

"You boys okay," Alan's father said in his deep baritone.

"Yup, we're fine, Dad," Alan said. "Can Victor sleep over?"

"Sure, just don't stay up too late," Alan's father said, then walked away from the door and back downstairs.

"Hope you don't mind," Alan said.

Victor gave Alan a playful punch on the arm. "Not one bit," he said.

MASETTO

I

"It's you! You've come back."

"No, not yet. I've come for answers."

"Answers?"

"Answers and the story. How it happened. I need to hear from you how it happened."

"But you know how it happened."

"Tell me."

"You know how. You were there."

"No, Loperello. I'm a stranger to you."

"But I knew you."

"You do not know me. Tell me as if you do not know me. You never knew me."

"But — "

"Never, Loperello. You never knew me."

"Okay. Okay. Sit back and I will tell you."

II

It was in the early twentieth century that I had met

Masetto. He'd been a priest back then, before he'd met up with me, but I'd known who he was far before we'd actually met. I had often spied upon him, watching him walk the cobbled streets of Rome in his black robe and collar. Being so handsome, Masetto always turned a few heads back then. Masetto's hair was dark and wavy, his jaw line prominent and defined. His hands were big, with long, thick fingers. When he took your hand in his you could feel his masculinity. Masetto's eyes, so dark and mysterious. Some men called them haunting, but not me. For me, nothing is haunting.

Masetto walking. Yes, that is how I remember him in the days before we'd met. Masetto walked with a surety that men often found appealing. To me, it was almost arrogant, the way he seemed to know every step, every inch of his travel. It was as if his destiny had already been told to him. But it hadn't been. Although I knew the truth about him, others did not. He would not have been successful with his flock if they'd known about him. If his flock had known the truth, they would not have followed him into the church the way they had. They would have had him tossed out, excommunicated. Those people he'd loved so desperately, the very souls he'd wanted to save, would have had him cast out of their lives, their religion, their very salvation. But, unlike me, they hadn't found out about him, so Masetto had never seen people at their worst. Perhaps if he had things would have turned out different. But then I wouldn't be here, telling you this now.

I first saw Masetto on a cool summer night as he walked down the cobbled streets of Rome in his robe and collar. A man of God he was, visiting church going men and women. What he didn't know was that I had visited those families with him. Hiding in shadows, I listened to Masetto talk about immortal souls and death as if he'd known about them from first hand experience. How captivating he was as he spoke, his hands gesturing as he walked about the small confines of the poor people of Rome. And as Masetto spoke, both men and women looked up at him as if in awe, hanging on his every word.

I'm sure they were merely entranced by his virile beauty, although they would never admit to such a thing. A man of the cloth was supposed to be sexless and pure. Such nonsense, actually. How can a man be sexless? Take a man's virility away from him and what is he? He is nothing. But that is only my opinion, based upon what I've seen and Masetto. Masetto, the one man whose life has touched mine like no other.

Masetto, handsome, arrogant and virile. Ah yes, a man of the cloth is supposed to be without virility. But that was his greatest weakness. Some would say that I'm wrong, that Masetto's downfall was his libido, not his virility. In some instances those people are right. It was Masetto's libido that often drew his hand to his cock while lying awake at night. How he'd fought his humanity, trying desperately not to give in to the urge to feel his skin, or touch his hardness. Many times I'd stood in the dark confines of his room, watching as he tossed and turned in bed, naked beneath a thin sheet on a wood cot with a thin mattress of feathers. I'd watched him toss off the sheet, seen his full naked form. Masetto's body, narrow and tight, with a dusting of hair on his upper chest and a small thin trail that reached down to the bush of dark hair just above his cock and balls. And it never took long for Masetto's hand to reach down and grab his stiff shaft once the covers had been tossed off.

Masetto's cock was nine inches when fully erect and so thick his fingers barely touched once he'd taken hold of it. The foreskin clung tight around the head, from which spilled copious amounts of clear, viscous pre-seminal fluid. Masetto liked to rub his palm over the head as it dripped the luscious fluids and use it to lubricate his shaft. Countless times I'd watched him perform this very act. I'd watched him spread his legs so his big hairy balls dropped down between them in their fleshy sack, falling upon the mattress as he stroked himself to completion.

And each time, after Masetto had cum, he'd kneel down beside his bed, clasp his hands together and pray for forgiveness. For Masetto had often taken part in that singular, libidinous pleasure. Masturbation, a pleasure the libido drives a person to enact. The libido, that sexual drive, the pressure between a man's legs that calls out to him for release. If only that alone had been enough to please Masetto, but it hadn't been enough. Masturbation only fueled his lust and brought out his deeper desires. Desires he hadn't been able to ignore on the nights he'd traveled out of Rome, to the outer towns and villages.

These were places where city life was unheard of, where farming was the main source of income. Sturdy, rugged men lived in these towns, tending fields and feeding livestock. These men had brawn and unshaven faces. Their hands were calloused from hard work. They were the men who worked long, hard hours in the fields and spent their evenings with friends. They were the men Masetto had longed to feel against his body. Masetto wanted to have their calloused hands rubbing his tender flesh and their stiff cocks in his mouth. He wanted to smell their bodies, have the scent of hard work fill his nostrils. How Masetto longed to feel their large, stiff poles buried deep inside his body, sliding in and out until they could no longer hold back. He wanted to be filled with their seed.

Every Saturday Masetto went out to the country. For him it was a day to himself, so he never wore his robes. All the priests and monks at the abbey knew about Masetto's Saturday pleasures of fresh air and sunshine, but none of them knew what really happened on those pleasant trips.

I spent most Friday nights following Masetto from the shadows where it seemed I lived. I listened in on his private conversations, at times getting the name of the village he was planning on visiting. Thankfully Masetto was quite gregarious, and was often asked what he was doing to occupy his time. Men were always mystified about how men of the cloth lived, and could never understand how a man like Masetto could live without sex. Very often they'd asked him how he was able to stay sane, to which Masetto's reply had always been : A day in the country does wonders. Oh yes, and wonders those Saturdays did.

I might have only been able to catch Masetto's nocturnal wanderings, but that had been enough to understand exactly who he was. For here is where Masseto's libido and virility meet. For the country is where the men he'd seen only in his fantasies lived. Masetto watched these men, feeling desire for them grow in his loins. Could Masetto let them be, as he was able to do in the city? No, he was a man who needed to explore and feel the camaraderie of men whose pleasures and company he enjoyed. He needed to bond with them, feel enriched by their strength. When he was with them, every ounce of Masetto's virility had to come into play.

The change in Masetto when he'd gone off for his Saturday excursions was amazing. Dressed in cotton pants and shirt, the sleeves rolled up, the top three bottons on the shirt undone to show a hint of chest hair. His walk the same, his manners unchanged. He'd walk down country roads, his dark eyes enticing men as he passed them on streets lit by the windows of store fronts, houses and restaurants. How sure of himself he was, how sexually provocative. Masetto's virility shone like a beacon on those nights. Those nights when men were everywhere, ready for the taking.

Saturday nights I would search for Masetto and find him in various positions: on his knees behind barns, pleasuring a farmer with his mouth, sprawled out on a bed of hay with thick cum splattered on his face, on his knees with his lips pressed against another man's asshole, leaning over a work bench while a burly farmer sticks his stiff cock up his ass. Oh, these were the nights when Masetto's libido and virility came together. The nights when Masetto could take what he wanted and feel like a man.

When Masetto returned to Rome he paid dearly for his desires. Saturday nights were pleasure, but Sunday nights were pain. And I know, for I stood in the dark recesses of his room and watched as Masetto knelt with his head bowed in prayer as he sent the leather strap in his right hand repeatedly against his back. With each blow a red stripe formed on his back, and with each red stripe a grunt of agony and the words, "forgive me father." Standing in shadow, unseen, I watched Masetto pay for his virility.

Humanity, I often thought as I walked around the room, watching his face contort in agony as the leather strap slapped painfully against his flesh. Strips of red welts rose on his back. Small pearls of deep red blood formed along the very edges of some of those strips of pain. What good was being human doing Masetto? I did not know then, nor will I ever understand.

But watching Masetto, seeing his naked body, his sexual appetite being sated, did bring rise to an inner sense I thought had long since departed from my being. A sense more like desire that could not be sated, which became longing.

How I longed to feel Masetto's body, touch his muscular form and grasp his stiffening shaft. The desire to kiss him, to feel his lips pressed against mine, took seed in my mind. Despite the passing of time, the feeling of a throbbing shaft filling my ass, or a swollen cock head in my mouth had risen to the surface. Desires that had laid dormant, Masetto awoke. Desires that I had not felt for centuries were coming to the surface. And as I looked upon Masetto's back, at the red, swollen stripes cutting his flesh, I longed to run my tongue along just one of them and taste him.

But I held back. I told myself no, that I couldn't. I could not go back. It would be impossible to feel the same swelling excitement as before. Particularly at that time, while he was racked with pain and self disgust. And so on those nights I stayed and watched Masetto's body take the beatings until he could take no more and slipped into bed to fall asleep.

Following Masetto was not all that took up my nights. My nocturnal pursuits also consisted of parks and alleyways, looking for something enticing for temporary excitement. Oftentimes I found young men in search of excitement and a fast buck. Handsome men willing to entice a wanderer into a secluded area for money. Oftentimes I went with them, behind bushes and trees, to spots where I was able to touch their warm flesh, dip my hand into their trousers and feel their stiff maleness. And how calm they'd all been, telling me to go on, to touch them and feel them while taking out a knife or a gun to threaten me.

So foolish, these men were. It had been a pleasure to look into their eyes and let them know that I was not going to stand for their games. They never got an ounce of money from me, but I always received plenty from them. How these men gasped when my fingers were thrust against their throats. The look in their wide eyes as they soon understood what it was that I wanted. For, at that point, I did not hide my true nature. They saw my pointed teeth, felt the coolness of my skin. Save for a cry, a plea or a whimper, they were all the same. Unlike Masetto, these men lived off the misfortunes of others. They took and did not give.

Masetto longed for a purity that does not exist in the world. A purity he could not find in himself, although he desired it. How my heart went out to him.

Every day, as I lie in slumber, my hands crossed and the scent of earth and silk filling my nostrils, I dreamt of Masetto. He filled my dreams and my mind with the desire to touch him. To feel my hand upon his flesh. How much I wanted to run my tongue along his salty skin and taste his body; feel his ass cheeks against my face, my tongue against his puckered asshole. How badly I wanted to wrap my arms around him, penetrate him and feel my shaft buried deep inside his body. The mere thought of feeling Masetto's ass ring gripping my shaft seemed to haunt my every thought, like a craving that would not go away until I was able to have one taste. And so that was what I was going to do. I would have my taste and be done with it.

So now you see, our fate had been sealed.

III

I waited for a weekend to take up my adventure with Masetto. I followed him on his nightly excursions, where he would often tell of his plans for the weekend. As always, he was going out to the country. He would be staying at a small inn called Giovanni's.

Friday night, dressed as a peasant, I wandered the countryside in search of Masetto. I found him leaving his room at Giovanni's Inn, taking in a breath of fresh night air, then rubbing his stomach. He wore a pullover top with an open collar, his pants were baggy and worn, as if he was indeed one of the townspeople. Masetto's shoes scuffed dirt into the air as he walked past open, moonlit fields. As always, he strode along with his hands in his pockets, whistling a soft tune.

Keeping on the grass, I stepped into view, then asked, "What is that tune you're whistling?"

Masetto stopped, then turned towards me. He looked startled, yet unafraid. "I thought I was alone," he said.

"I was out for a stroll on the grass when I heard your whistling. It's a lovely tune."

"It's something I made up," Masetto said, looking past me.

"It must be nice to be musical."

Masetto didn't listen, instead he looked out and said, "Why didn't I see you? You were out in the fields, but I never saw you."

"I was much further back," I said, then watched as my words sunk in.

"Behind me," Masetto said, then looked me over. His eyes lingered on the bulge of cock between my legs.

"I was out for a walk. It's such a calm night. There was no way I could pass it up."

"Perfect for a walk," Masetto said, his eyes not leaving mine. "I know a quiet place, if you want to join me."

My shaft stiffened even more as I took him up on the offer, then walked across the fields. He took me to an abandoned farm house. The fields were burnt by the sun and the soil was dry. Masetto told me what a shame he thought it was for such a nice piece of property to go to waste. He took me into the barn, where a shaft of moonlight spilled in from the open hayloft door and filled the open interior with a dim yellow glow. The subtle, soft human scent of Masetto's body filled the room, enticing me to search out his flesh.

Between his legs, Masetto's manhood bugled out long and hard down his left thigh. I walked up to him, reached out and held the bulge of meat in my hand. Masetto let out a soft gasp as I felt the thick fleshy tube through the thin cotton of his pants. Quickly, I unfastened the buttons and dipped my fingers inside his fly.

"Your hands are cold," Masetto said as I took his manhood in my hand.

"They'll heat up," I said, sliding my free hand beneath his shirt. His left nipple stiffened as the tip of my index finger passed it. I kissed his neck, tasting the salt of his skin on my lips.

"Are you ill?" Masetto asked as he tried to push away from me.

"Please, Masetto," I said, reaching around his torso and pulling him close. My right hand slipped out from under his shirt and slid up behind him.

Masetto's eyes grew wide, his breathing hastened. "My

name!" he called out "You know my name."

He tried to push me away once more, but I was too quick for him. From behind, I took hold of a lock of his hair and jerked his head to the side. My tongue ran along his neck, lapping up the taste of him as small bumps rose on his flesh.

"You're so cold," Masetto said frantically as he squirmed in my grasp.

"I've been wanting you for so long, Masetto," I said, wrapping my left arm around his torso and holding him close. "Just to touch you, feel your body close to mine. To touch your flesh and sink my manhood deep inside your body."

"Let me go, please," Masetto pleaded.

My tongue gently traveled over his full lips.

"Who are you?" Masetto asked, a tinge of concern evident in his voice.

"Loperello," I said, smiling enough to show my fangs.

Masetto's eyes grew wide as he let out a gasp.

"Do not fear me," I said softly. I bent down and kissed his neck, then felt his body stiffen in my grasp. Holding him close, I let my hand travel from his back to the rounded curve of his ass.

"I've seen you with other men," I whispered into Masetto's ear. "I've seen you take their manhood in your mouth and your ass. You swallowed their seed and had it sprayed on your face."

"What do you want from me?" Masetto asked.

"Put your hands between my legs and find out," I said.

Masetto looked into my eyes and I let him go, but he did not take a step away from me. He held my stare.

Holding out my hands, I said, "Touch it."

Masetto looked at my form, then slowly moved his trembling hand towards my crotch. He took hold of my sex and caressed it through its cloth confines. The heat from his touch warmed my cock and balls, making my shaft shift and grow. Without looking away, Masetto unbuttoned my pants and slipped his hand inside. He pulled out my meat, then looked down at it. Ten inches of thick cock was in his grip. He wrapped his fingers around the shaft, but his fingertips did not touch.

"It's so big," Masetto said as he looked down at it. He slid has hand down to slide the foreskin back and expose the pale knob.

Placing my hands on his shoulders, I guided him down on his knees. His hot, moist tongue ran along the length of my cock, then around the sensitive head. His warm, moist tongue slid along the lower side of my prick as he swallowed my length.

Taking hold of my pole, Masetto stroked it and watched the pale, bulbous head. He wrapped his lips around it and continued to suck. As much as he did, I knew he would never get the outcome he so desired. But if only, I thought. If only I could. How beautiful it would be to cover Masetto's handsome face with my cream.

"Not yet," I said softly. "Get up and let me see your naked body."

Masetto stood, then slowly lifted his shirt over his head, exposing his broad, muscular chest. He stepped out of his shoes and unfastened his pants as I did the same.

I looked at Masetto, at the soft ripple of musculature beneath his flesh. His cock stood erect, reaching up to his navel. A hood of flesh covered the lower half of the head of his dick, and a bead of clear pre-seminal fluid glistened on the tip. His legs were tight with muscle, matching every ounce of his male form.

Walking around him, I studied his firm ass. I reached out and separated his ass cheeks to study his tight hole. His pucker tightened and winked at me as I went down on my knees and gave it a kiss. The heavy, musty scent of his ass filled my nostrils, tantalizing my senses and arousing my passions once more. Dragging my tongue up the crack of his ass, then along his spine, I slowly rose to my feet.

Masetto pressed his ass against my shaft, burying my stiffness between his firm ass cheeks. Kissing his neck, I began to rub my hardness against his body, feeling the heat of his form. Reaching around with my right hand, I took hold of Masetto's cock and began to stroke it. His breathing became heavy as I kissed his neck, feeling the pulse of life run through his body.

"Stick it in me," Masetto called out as he pushed his ass out, against my cock.

I continued to stroke his shaft. Masetto let out a sigh as I gently nibbled on his neck. The urge to feed began to grow stronger as I stroked his shaft. His head tilted back, onto my shoulder. I held the tip of my tongue against his flesh, feeling the blood move through his vein.

"Please," Masetto whispered as he reached behind himself and lowered my cock between his legs.

Fighting my inhuman need, I gripped Masetto's fleshy staff and continued to slide my hand up and down it. I clenched my jaw and rubbed my cock against Masetto's moist hole.

Masetto's breathing continued. The blood in his body seemed to pound in my ears. Masetto's life was in my hands. I gripped his shaft, then kissed his neck.

"Please," Masetto called out, his voice soft and heavy.

His salty flesh was there, ready for me to take. I told myself not to do it, but he was there, willing.

"Do it, please," Masetto said, his breathing even heavier than before. He let out a deep groan as every muscle in his body tensed, then I sunk my teeth quickly into his body. Masetto called out in pain as a blast of hot semen burst from his dick.

I pulled my teeth out of his flesh as hot, thick red liquid pulsed out of his body and filled my mouth. Masetto tried to fight, but it was no use. I had already wrapped one arm around his mid-section and used the other to hold his head still.

"Don't kill me, please," Masetto said.

I kissed the tender wounds I'd inflicted upon him, then ran the flat of my tongue over them. Masetto's blood raced through my body, giving me strength from its nourishment.

How shocked I'd been by what I had done to Masetto. I hadn't intended to harm him. I had only wanted to feel his body against mine, touch him the way I had never touched another man's body. But now his life was leaving him as I held him in my arms. He didn't want to die, nor had I intended to kill him. Leaning down, I pressed my lips against the holes in his neck and continued to drink.

When Masetto's body was near death, his heart beating so slow that it was almost undecipherable, I released him. Masetto's body fell to the ground at my feet. His face beheld the most beautiful mix of fear and arousal that I had ever seen. Rising up hard between his legs was his cock, cum still dripping from the piss slit.

Through pale, lifeless eyes, Masetto looked up at me, searching my face as if for meaning. Holding my wrist up to my mouth, I bit into my skin and drew blood. Masetto's parched lips quivered as I held my wrist over them and let the deep red liquid spill into his mouth. I let more fall between his lips and waited for him to drink on his own. And when he did, he took hold of my wrist as if he would not let go. Greedily he drank, sucking long and hard.

When I pulled my wrist away from Masetto's mouth, he growled, then his body began to convulse. With each convulsion, his cock twitched and spurt thick globs of creamy spunk that covered his chest and stomach in what would be his final orgasm.

Sweat came on as color drained from his body, turning his deep complexion to an ashen white. He turned towards me, eyes wide in fright, his lips trembling. He could not speak, although I knew he wanted to. Then his body cramped, and he quickly slid into a fetal position and vomited all that he had consumed during the day.

For Masetto the journey away from the mortal coil he'd known so well must have taken an eternity, but it was nothing more than twenty minutes. I stood by and watched, amazed at the mystical beauty of the event. The waxing of color and expelling of mortal excrement. I watched as Masetto's body began a new life.

When Masetto's body rested from its departure, I took him to my temporary dwellings, washed him, then placed him in an extra casket to rest out the daylight hours. He looked so peaceful lying there, naked, hands over his stomach, eyes closed.

What I would tell him the following night I did not know, nor did I care to ponder it. All I wanted was to rest, and that was what I did.

IV

The following night Masetto awoke. He was weak and confused as he lifted himself up from the confines of his resting place. A wrought iron candelabra stood on the floor in the far corner of the room, it's four arms rising towards the ceiling in various stages. On each arm rested a pillar candle that helped set the room aglow in a flickering light. Masetto stood on shaky legs and looked around the room; at the small table, a sofa, two chairs and two coffins.

"What have you done with me?" Masetto asked, his chest heaving as if fighting for air. He ran across the room to the heavily draped window. He pulled open the drapes only to find that the window had been boarded up.

"Nobody has lived here for years," I told him, standing in the center of the room. "For us it's only temporary. Once you have all your strength we will move."

Masertto's feet slapped the floor as he lunged at me. He

grabbed hold of my shirt and tried to push me against the wall, but his strength had already failed him. I tossed him back as if he were an old shirt. Masetto fell back onto the floor. Looking up at me, he asked once more what I had done to him.

I said nothing.

"What have you done to me?" Masetto hissed.

"Give it time and you will find out on your own," I said with a grin, although I knew it to be wrong.

Leaving Masetto locked inside, I went into the city to find a tasty treat. I walked the busy streets of Rome looking into alleys and bars, searching for the perfect man to take. Casually I walked down the streets to the sounds of horse hooves, wheels against cobble stones and men on foot. Some of the men caught my eye, but I let them pass. I still hadn't decided how it was that I would handle getting the victim back to Masetto. It was then that I spotted the man I wanted sitting atop a carriage, reins resting in front of him. His hat was by his side and his head tilted back as if looking at the night sky.

"It's amazing, isn't it, the sky," I said to him, looking up at him from the street.

The driver looked down at me, his thin lips forming a slight grin that let me know he was old enough to understand the desires of men. He said, "Some things can never be figured out."

"And other things need to be explored to be understood," I said, giving him my best devilish grin and a seductive wink.

He smiled back at me, then turned towards me as if getting ready for a lengthy discussion.

"Have you long to wait?" I asked.

"Yes, I do," he said. "Why do you ask?"

"I've never seen the interior of one of these carriages before."

The driver hoisted himself down from his perch, then

opened the carriage door for me to enter. We situated ourselves side by side on the bench, then the driver closed the curtains that hung on the windows. He placed his hand on my thigh, then looked into my eyes.

I smiled back at him and placed my hand between his legs, feeling his bulging meat, then gave him a light kiss on the lips. Dipping my hand inside his trousers, I took hold of his fleshy mast, then kissed his neck. The driver slid back in the seat and let out a soft breath. As he came closer to orgasm, his breathing heightened and his pulse quickened. With my lips closed, I found the place on his neck where the blood flowed most, then sank my teeth. He let out a gasp, then I felt my mouth become flooded with his life.

I drained him until he went pale and could no longer move. His heart still pumped what little blood was left in him, which I had left for Masetto. Using the driver's shirt, I wiped my mouth, then got out and positioned myself atop the carriage. I placed his hat upon my head and the reins in my hands. Off we drove, to see Masetto.

Still naked, Masetto was sprawled on the sofa when I carried the body to him. Beads of perspiration dotted Masetto's brow, and he looked weak and ashen. Turning his head away, Masetto told me to take the body away.

"You need to feed, Masetto," I said, laying the body on the floor. "You're growing weak."

Maesetto turned toward me, his eyes wide and furious. "What have you done to me, Loperello? Answer me!"

"I only wanted to feel you, not take you like this," I said, sitting next to him. I tried to take his hand, but he quickly moved it away.

Standing on shaky legs, Masetto looked down at the body. Masetto's nostrils flared, taking in the scent of life about leave a body, then he turned towards me as if about to ask a question.

"You must take him before he passes on," I said.

Masetto fell to his knees beside the body, leaning over him as if to talk to him. He rolled him onto his back and saw the life in his open eyes. The man's lips began to move, and Masetto leaned in as if to hear what he had to say. Masetto's arms began to shake with hunger and need as he looked over the body beneath him. He stayed still for a moment, then lunged at the neck and greedily ate.

"Not all of it," I said, walking over to where he fed. I pulled Masetto away from the body.

Blood smeared Masetto's mouth and chin as he looked up at me. He turned towards the blood smeared neck of the body on the floor as it died, then took three steps back.

"What hell have you taken me to?" he asked, his voice thunderously loud.

"There is no Hell," I said. "Holy water will not boil your skin, nor will a cross burn you. This is the only afterlife there is. This is all you ever had."

Masetto turned to me, his eyes blazing with hate. "You fool!"

"This is all you ever had, Masetto."

"I had so much more. So much that you will never understand."

"And *now* you have so much more."

"I have nothing! Look at me, Loperello. You have taken all that I am away. Everything! And for what?" Masetto said as he grabbed his clothes from the table and began to dress.

"Eternal life," I said.

Stopping as he buttoned his trousers, Masetto looked up at me. "Eternal life? Like this?"

"There is no other way."

"You lie," Masetto hissed as he continued to dress. When he'd finished, he went to the door, then outside.

I followed him down the dimly lit, cobbled streets of

Rome, past tall stone buildings and store front windows. It was obvious where he was going, but what he would do when he arrived was unclear. In his country attire nobody seemed to recognize him, but Masetto didn't seem to mind. He had a mission, and it seemed that nothing would stop him from achieving it.

Standing across the street from the rectory where he once lived, he stared up at the window that was once his room. I don't know what was going through his mind then, but he seemed sad and lost. To the left of the rectory was the stone front of St. Sebastian's looming up in a peak flanked by two stone turrets. Masetto ran up the stone steps and stood in front of the double doors at the entrance. Reaching out, he slowly took hold of the brass rings that were the handles, opened the double doors and walked inside.

Keeping to the darkest corners, I watched as he cautiously dipped his fingers into the holy water, then made the sign of the cross as he mumbled the words he'd known his entire life: In the name of the Father, the Son and Holy Ghost. Slowly, he walked down the red carpet, past hundreds of pews, statues of saints and the arched stain glass windows depicting the stations of the cross on either side. Masetto's soft sobs echoed against the stone walls of the vacant church as he made his way to the altar, where Jesus hung on the cross, his tilted head looking down at him. Falling to his knees, Masetto clasped his hands in prayer and looked up at the looming figure of Jesus.

Footsteps echoed from the distance, then a man of the cloth appeared in the doorway to the left of the altar. Masetto looked up at the man, then stood.

"Masetto, where have you been?" the man asked.

"Please, Ottavio, you must help me. I am so lost," Masetto said. With his hands clasped in prayer, he knelt and lowered his upper torso to the floor while his body shook with anguished sobs.

"Do you have something to confess?" Ottavio asked.

Masetto's breathing became heavy as he looked up at Ottavio. "Get away from me!" he called out.

Ottavio went down on his knees and grasped Masetto's shoulders. He looked into Masetto's eyes and said, "You have been gone so long, Masetto. Tell me what is wrong. Are you in trouble?"

"Such trouble, Ottavio! Bless me! Do what you can to free me from this torment."

"You must confess," Ottavio said.

What little blood I had consumed that night began to fill my shaft as Masetto looked deep into Ottavio's eyes, their lips so close to touching. Masetto looked weak and hungry, desperately holding himself back from his deepest need. Rubbing my fleshy rod, I watched as Masetto's tongue gently caressed Ottavio's full lips.

Ottavio kissed him back.

"I know of your anguish," Ottavio said.

Unbuttoning my pants, I reached into the opening and took my stiffness in hand. Slowly stroking my shaft, I watched as Masetto wrapped his arms around Ottavio's body and buried his face against his neck. Ottavio let out a gasp, then gripped Masetto's form. I continued to play with my shaft as Masetto drank from Ottavio, nourishing his body with the life of another. And when he'd finished, he rose to his knees, his mouth red with blood. Masetto's sobs echoed inside the church, filling it with his loss.

It was then that he knew what he was.

V

"Such nonsense, Loperello! Who are you to say what I felt or knew back then, a century ago? Did you ever see me again after that night?"

"No, I did not."

"Then how can you say such a thing? You do not

understand that you took away more than my belief, you stole my desire. A desire that no man or belief can take from another, you took from me. My need to touch another man's body and respond in kind has been taken away. You know nothing of the misery I felt wandering the world, seeking out men to fulfill more than just my hunger. Do you understand that, Loperello?"

"I just told you my story, was that not enough?"

"Half a story, that's all you told me. The half that sought me out and took me away from a world I knew too well and did not want to leave. And for what? Nothing but a simple pleasure you can't even feel."

"But I wanted you, Masetto. How I longed to touch you and feel more than your blood filling my body. How I longed to feel once more what it is to have fresh semen filling my shaft, pulsing out of the head. You don't understand how strong my desire was. How alone I felt. What it is to desire something you cannot have."

"The ecstacy. I once knew that desire. I spent the last century traveling the world, feeling hot cum spit out of cocks, onto my face. Thick warmth dripping down my nose, off my chin. The heady scent of sweaty balls filling my nostrils, forcing me to long for a sensation I can no longer feel. An ecstacy that is not mine."

"I should have never made you."

"It's too late for regrets, Loperello. When you took me, you sent me to a world of darkness. A place where passion goes unfulfilled. I must live with that, as must you. We are too much alike now."

"But —"

"No buts."

"Masetto, please, try to understand."

"Understand what? That you longed to feel a lust that was no longer yours and that was why you made me? Tell me, is that what I must understand?"

"My hunger was too strong, Masetto. I could not stop my true nature."

"Your true nature. Please, Loperello! Your true nature gave me a life of darkness. A life where I can only live alone. I cannot find any others like us."

"You don't know where to look."

"There are none of us."

"They will not come out to you like this. You must accept what you are."

"I must accept that I am alone, is that what you ask of me? That is something I already know. Loneliness fills my nights, takes me in and holds me close. I no longer want it, Loperello."

"What do you want?"

"I want what I cannot have."

"Death?"

"Sensation. Ecstacy. Desire."

"Then let me hold you. Let me touch your naked body, feel your ivory skin, and taste your lifeless form. Let me feel your cool lips upon mine."

"And what good will that do me?"

"Come, Masetto. Let me hold you. Perhaps then you will find out."

"Is this a trick?"

"No tricks. Come. Relax. Relax and let me touch your body. Relax and accept."

"I cannot relax, nor will I accept what has become of me."

"But —"

"I came for answers, that is all. Now I must go."

"But where, Masetto? Stay here with me."

"Stay with you and live in folly? Never. I will roam the Earth and hope for a death that will never come, no matter how much I pray.

Because of you, Loperello, I am filled with self loathing for an eternity. Because of you I will never have the chance to mend my ways and be forgiven. I must live with this self hatred for all eternity."

"That is not true, Masetto."

"Look at me, Loperello! Look at me! I am what no man should ever be."

about the author

Kenneth Harrison is also the author of two collections of short stories and the novels *Bad Behavior* and *Lies and Deceptions*. His short stories have also been included in the anthologies *Butch Boys* and *Grave Passions*. He lives a quiet life in Providence, RI. For a full list of his publishing credits visit him on the web at http://www.KennethHarrison.com